How to Spot a Murder Plot

A MAGS AND BIDDY GENEALOGY MYSTERY BOOK FOUR

ELIZA WATSON

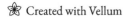

Books by Eliza Watson

NONFICTION

Genealogy Tips & Quips

FICTION

A Mags and Biddy Genealogy Mystery Series

How to Fake an Irish Wake (Book 1)

How to Snare a Dodgy Heir (Book 2)

How to Handle an Ancestry Scandal (Book 3)

How to Spot a Murder Plot (Book 4)

How to Trace a Cold Case (Book 5)

The Travel Mishaps of Caity Shaw Series

Flying by the Seat of My Knickers (Book 1)

Up the Seine Without a Paddle (Book 2)

My Christmas Goose Is Almost Cooked (Book 3)

My Wanderlust Bites the Dust (Book 4)

Live to Fly Another Day (Book 5)

When in Doubt Don't Chicken Out (Book 6)

FOR ADDITIONAL BOOKS VISIT

WWW.ELIZAWATSON.COM.

Dear Reader,

In *How to Spot a Murder Plot*, Mags and Biddy travel to Scotland for a family reunion. I chose to set this story in Scotland rather than in Ballycaffey, Ireland, because Scotland is my Watsons' homeland and holds a special place in my heart.

My grandpa Watson's father abandoned him when he was two years old, so we had no knowledge of our Watson family history. We always thought Watson sounded English, so we'd assumed our family had emigrated from England. After years of extensive research, I traced our Watsons back from Chicago to Kingston, Ontario, to Montreal, Quebec, and finally to Glasgow, Scotland. In 2018 I visited my Watsons' homeland and thought it would be fun to set a book there. I hope you enjoy your trip to Scotland with Mags and Biddy. No matter what country these two lasses are in, there is sure to be plenty of shenanigans!

At the end of this story, I've included three research articles. Two articles are from my nonfiction book, *Genealogy Tips & Quips*: "Truth or Dare: Are You Prepared for Your DNA Test Results?" and "Family Reunions: More than Potluck and Playing Cards." One tip is from my December 2021 newsletter: "Researching Scottish Ancestors in Ireland and Irish Ancestors in Scotland." I hope my tips inspire you to begin tracing your family tree or help you break down a brick wall you've been beating your head against for months or years!

Cheers!
Eliza Watson

To my dad, Douglas Watson, and our ancestor James Watson, who emigrated from Glasgow, Scotland. Also, to living Scottish relations I hope to find someday.

Glossary

Several characters in this book use English, Irish, and Scottish terms and slang. This glossary might help you learn a few new words and phrases you can use to impress your friends.

aye: Yes.
bairn: Small child.
belter: An outstanding person or event.
biscuit: Cookie.
bonnie: Beautiful.
braw: Grand or lovely.
buttery: A round flaky pastry similar to a croissant. Also known as a rowie or Aberdeen roll.
clan: A clan describes a close-knit group of relatives. However, anyone who pledged their allegiance to the chief could use the clan's name, including those who worked for the clan or needed protection. A clan often included numerous septs—families with other surnames. Clans were associated with a geographical area of Scotland.

craic: To have fun. *Last night was great craic.* It may also be used as a greeting. *How's the craic?*

crisps: Potato chips.

cuppa: Cup of tea.

daftie: Fool.

dram: A drink of whiskey or other liquor.

eejit: Idiot.

fag: Cigarette.

gob: Mouth.

gobshite: Idiot.

haggis: National dish of Scotland.

hen: Woman.

Janey/Janey Mac: Exclamation of surprise or concern.

lassie: Girl.

loo: Bathroom.

maw: Mother.

Mirrie Dancers: Northern lights.

muppet: Fool.

nay: No.

nick: Steal.

off your/my trolley: Off your/my rocker.

peely-wally: Looking under the weather or pale. Often used after someone spent a night out drinking.

pet: A term of endearment, such as "dear" or "sweetie."

pinch: Steal.

shag: To have sex.

sláinte: Cheers.

solicitor: Lawyer.

tartan: A woolen cloth woven in one of several patterns of plaid, especially a design associated with a particular Scottish clan.

tattie: Potato.

uni: University.

wally: Foolish person.

wee: A small amount or a young person. However, this term is used frequently even if not referring to either. *Would you fancy a wee cup of tea?* However, the beverage could be served in a large mug rather than a dainty little teacup.

yoke: A term that is interchangeable with the word "thing."

One

HEART RACING, I touched my foot cautiously on the ground, debating the safest path to take. My breathing quickened. A brisk fall breeze whipped my long hair across my face and filled my head with the scent of dried leaves and damp earth, along with thoughts of...the dead.

"A lovely bouquet of berries and black currant would taste grand right now." My best friend, Biddy McCarthy, tapped a black flat impatiently against a toppled-over headstone buried in the tall grass. "We must crack on. Off to the dungeon to visit the living. The welcome reception has already started."

Dusk settling in, I peered around Dalwade Castle's graveyard, wanting to savor my first visit to a Scottish cemetery. Colorful leaves clung to life on the towering oaks' swaying limbs. Ivy wrapped around weathered tombstones and trailed along the surrounding stone fence and an abandoned medieval church. The landscape of Celtic crosses resembled an Irish cemetery. I let out a contented sigh, feeling right at home.

"I'm sure the castle has a list of everyone buried here," Biddy said.

"What fun is that? I didn't research the cemetery in advance so I could experience the thrill of the unknown. The names, dates, and memorials slowly materializing as you mold aluminum foil against a two-hundred-year-old headstone."

"Come back tomorrow when you're better dressed for traipsing through a cemetery and I'm wrapped in a fluffy spa robe." Biddy carefully removed a prickly burr from her navy tights and brushed several dried leaves from her short red, green, and yellow plaid skirt. The McCarthy tartan pattern. Biddy was Irish but in the Scottish spirit.

The Murray tartan inspired my blue, green, and red plaid skirt. My dad was descended from Clan Murray of Atholl in the Scottish Highlands. Two years ago a DNA test revealed that I wasn't descended from the clan or Scottish. My dad wasn't my biological father, it turned out. A secret my mom had taken to her grave nearly four years ago. Thanks to Ancestry.com recently providing more precise ethnicity estimates, my Irish and English percentages decreased 8 percent, and Scottish materialized. My grandpa Fitzsimmons's line had distant ties to Scotland.

Ethnicity estimates were exactly that. Estimates.

Yet now I could boast having Scottish in my DNA!

"I'm not about to be twisting an ankle or disappearing into a sinkhole at my first Scottish castle," Biddy said.

She was still a bit traumatized about her foot having slipped into a grave when she was ten.

"Just let me take a quick look at that grave over there." The massive tombstone nearer the church must have been for someone important, like Lord Kerr, who'd built the castle in 1492. I placed a foot lightly on the uneven ground before putting weight on it, leaves crackling under my black flat.

Biddy trailed cautiously behind me through the tall grass, groaning in protest.

A distressed moan came from inside the abandoned church. Biddy and I exchanged surprised glances. Had a stone tumbled from the wall and hit someone exploring the ruins?

"Oh...Malcolm..." A woman's breathless voice stopped us in our tracks.

"Eeewww," Biddy whispered. "Who has sex inside a deserted church?"

Likely a relative of my dad's, since the Murray reunion had bought out the castle hotel's twenty-two guest rooms.

"Malcolm!" another woman called out in the distance.

My gaze darted to the dirt path leading through the cemetery's wrought iron gate to the formal garden.

The moaning ceased.

Biddy and I ducked behind a towering headstone.

"Are you out here?" the woman yelled from the garden.

Cussing and rustling sounds replaced the moans of ecstasy as the couple apparently scrambled to put themselves together.

Biddy and I quirked intrigued brows.

"I swear if you don't tell her, I will," the woman spat in an English accent. "I'm done shagging in public loos, cars, and now graveyards. I'm not some twit you picked up in a dance club."

Loos? Biddy mouthed.

"Izzy, it's you I love." The man's Scottish brogue

reminded me of the actor Gerard Butler. "Not much longer, I promise." A cell phone rang inside the church. "Coming, luv!" he yelled out.

"What a snake," I whispered.

The church door creaked open, and a man bolted out, fingers combing his rustled dark hair and pulling down the sleeves on his blue sweater. A minute later a woman appeared, adjusting her bra under a formfitting emerald-green dress. She huffed off in a pair of low-heeled tan pumps, long auburn curls bouncing against her back. I couldn't help but be impressed that she was able to navigate the uneven ground and fallen headstones in heels.

"What a bloody jerk," Biddy spat. "Have half a mind to tell that other woman, likely his wife, exactly what that bloke is up to."

"Since that bloody cad is likely a rellie, we'll keep our yaps shut. We're here to meet the Murrays, not cause family drama."

A growl vibrated at the back of Biddy's throat. "Fine."

We traipsed through the long grass, out the cemetery's gate, and down the dirt path. We crossed over a quaint stone bridge with a gurgling creek below, then through an ivy-wrapped trellis into the garden. Biddy tightened her signature blond ponytail. Having arrived at the hotel an hour late due to a delayed flight, I'd also gone for the ponytail look.

A dirt path cut through the garden's maze of hedges and flowering shrubs to the red brick castle now housing Dalwade Hotel and Spa. Narrow vertical slits lined the top of the corner towers and exterior walkways, where skilled archers once launched defensive arrows at their enemies.

A nervous fluttering rose from my stomach into my

chest. "Remember, don't mention I'm a genealogist. People might expect me to have traced the Murray family tree back ten generations. Or even worse, ask me to share my DNA profile and research."

Biddy saluted me. "Got it."

"It's nobody's business that I'm a skeleton in the Murray family closet. We're here to have fun, not be the source of everyone's gossip. Even though I'm not biologically a Murray, they are still my family."

Biddy jerked a thumb over her shoulder in the direction of the cemetery. "I certainly hope that wasn't part of our *fun*."

Biddy would be spending free time in the spa while I checked out cemeteries within a half-hour walking distance.

I grasped an iron handle and heaved open the castle's massive wooden door. We stepped inside, and the door shut behind us with a low boom, echoing down the corridor. Iron chandeliers lined the ceiling, and candle flames flickered in iron sconces along the hallway's stone walls. Swords, a coat of armor, antique tapestries, and the Kerr family crest added to the medieval ambiance. I envisioned Queen Victoria and Prince Albert walking across the same stone floor when they'd visited the castle in 1848.

Biddy admired a glass case displaying an antique arrow with a worn steel tip and a brown feather on the other end. "According to this plaque, the arrow was used by a famous archer who inspired the legend of Robin Hood. How cool is that?"

I envisioned Robin Hood shooting the arrow at men on the castle's towers defending the king's riches, while the hero fought for the rights of Nottingham's peasant population.

We continued on to the enclosed stairway leading down to the deep recesses of the castle.

"I should have taken a few archery lessons to prepare for the team-building event tomorrow," Biddy said. "What if I accidentally shoot a hawk or falcon flying over from the castle's falconry? Besides feeling horrible, if they're endangered, I might get fined and kicked out of the hotel. Then I'll be needing a massage more than ever."

"I doubt you're going to be able to shoot that high your first time. Besides, the birds are certainly trained to remain in their own airspace away from rogue arrows, or their survival instincts would surely kick in."

We exited the staircase into a narrow passageway. A chill slithered over me from a drop in temperature and thoughts of the poor souls who'd walked that same path to their imprisonment and likely deaths. Now, lively chatter filled the dungeon, where several dozen guests mingled at cabaret-style tables draped in Scottish-blue linens with white overlays. Elderly guests occupied blue satin-covered chairs at two cocktail tables. A tall young man dressed in a blue vest and black pants stood behind a small wooden bar tucked in a corner. Arched alcoves in the stone walls displayed silver trays with appetizers. The scent of garlic and melted butter made my stomach growl.

"I'm glad it's a bit bigger than I expected." Biddy peered over at a smaller attached room where a few people mingled. "Lord Kerr must have planned on imprisoning a lot of enemies."

Biddy occasionally suffered from claustrophobia. Like the time we'd somehow gotten locked in a bathroom at a Dublin restaurant. Before I could embarrass us by banging on the door for help, Biddy hopped up onto the sink and scrambled out a window into a sketchy alley. We reentered through the front door, where the hostess gave us a curious look.

A pretty middle-aged woman with a blond pixie haircut approached us. A Murray tartan–patterned shawl draped fashionably around her shoulders complemented her blue dress. Her gaze narrowed on Biddy's and my plaid skirts and matching black flats we'd bought for a steal last minute.

"So sorry. I didn't hire entertainment for the reception," she said with a Scottish lilt. "However, I do appreciate your attention to detail, wearing the Murray tartan. A very nice touch indeed."

Entertainment? It wasn't as if Biddy was wearing her blond curly step-dancing wig.

"Ah, actually, I'm Mags Murray. That's my dad, Ryan Murray. The tall dark-haired gentleman with a touch of gray in the blue wool blazer and Murray tartan tie." I gave Dad a wave across the room, where he was chatting with a woman in a tan dress who had my same chestnut-colored hair.

The blond woman's cheeks flushed pink with embarrassment. "Gads. So sorry about that. I recognize your name from the registration."

I smiled. "No worries."

She introduced herself as Ava Murray, the sister of the three men who'd visited us years ago in Chicago. Dad's second cousins, who shared great-grandparents in common with him. Dad's grandparents had emigrated from Scotland to the Chicago area shortly after marrying. I'd never known them, and his parents had died when I was in high school. Dad's brother had worked in Canada's remote oil fields forever. I'd only met him twice. At my Murray grandparents' funerals. This reunion would give us the perfect opportunity to bond with extended family.

"Grab yourselves a wee bevvy and join us," Ava said.

I pointed toward the bar, and Dad responded with a wink before returning to his conversation.

"Can't believe she thought we were bloody dancers," Biddy said.

"I can." I tugged the band from my hair and let it fall into a limp mess. "Not even one man is wearing a traditional kilt."

"The invite said dress for the occasion. What were we supposed to wear to a reception in a Scottish dungeon? Shackles and chains we picked up at some adult toy store?"

I nodded. "It should have been more specific." I was rethinking our outfits for the archery event tomorrow morning.

We ordered red wine served in pewter glasses with the Kerr family crest. Fancy.

"Sláinte."

We toasted to what was sure to be a memorable trip. It had to be better than my Canary Islands vacation with the McCarthys, when I suffered my worst sunburn ever. Or the time at Tayto Park when I'd puked all over everyone on the roller coaster.

We joined Dad's group, and a cool menthol scent filled my head, reminding me of Grandpa Murray. He'd always smelled like pain-reliever rub for his arthritis. Dad ran three miles every morning and was in terrific shape for being fifty-three years old. I doubted that he'd exchanged his musk cologne for eau de Ben Gay.

Ava introduced us to her brother Malcolm's wife, Rhona, an English woman.

Malcolm the cheating snake?

Biddy and I took a gulp of wine rather than ratting out Rhona's husband. Poor woman.

"I'm trying to talk your father into reactivating his DNA test on Ancestry.com," Ava said. "Might help me track down a line of Murrays who immigrated to Canada."

Dad had deactivated his test the day I'd received my DNA results and discovered my mom's secret.

"I told her I'd merely done it to learn my ethnicities," Dad said. "Not really into the whole DNA thing."

"But if it'll help her, why not?" I said.

Dad smiled, a flicker of hesitation in his blue eyes.

I nodded it was fine. Not being related to me, Ava couldn't view my DNA account and see Dad and I weren't a match. No reason for him not to share his results. Being a genealogist, I knew what it was like to desperately need close DNA matches to help solve family mysteries.

Ava smiled wide. "Brilliant. I recently received my DNA results and can't wait to dive into research." She turned to me. "Have you taken a test?"

I shook my head. "Sorry." I quickly diverted the topic. "As a family historian, you must be anxious to explore the castle's cemetery."

Ava nodded. "I spent a wee bit of time in it when Rhona and I were looking at hotels for the reunion. Now with the event kicking off, we've been spending all our time making sure everything is flawless."

Rhona smiled. "Yes, spending a night at five different castles was rough, but somebody had to do it."

"Having seen dozens of guest rooms, I can be fiercely jealous that Rhona and Malcolm are staying in the Queen Victoria Suite."

"Oh, wow," I said. "How awesome to sleep in the same bed as the queen once did."

Rhona nodded, blushing, appearing embarrassed that her sister-in-law had disclosed that she and her cheating husband were forking out four hundred pounds, almost six hundred bucks per night, to live like royalty. I was merely thrilled to be walking the same halls as the famous queen once had.

"It's a different mattress, I should hope." Rhona smiled. "You're welcome to stop by and see the suite. It's quite lovely. We could take tea in the sitting room."

"Sitting room?" Biddy said. "We barely have space to *sit* in our room unless it's on the bed."

Which felt like it was indeed the same mattress from two centuries ago stuffed with straw. The castle was a bit short on luxuries, but it was big on character.

"We're staying in Euphemia's Quarters," Biddy said. "The former servant's room where Lord Kerr supposedly impregnated the poor woman who bore his only son. She became his wife after his first wife suspiciously died."

When Biddy had decided to join Dad and me on the trip, we were lucky the room had opened up.

"It's very quaint," I assured Ava. "And I doubt that the average servant had a top-floor room with an incredible view."

A view of the tower's defensive wall more than the scenic surroundings, yet still a view.

The dark-haired handsome gentleman from the cemetery

joined us, slipping an arm around his wife's waist. His mistress glared at the couple from across the small room, where she was enjoying a drink with two elderly men.

"Is my sister boring you to death talking about dead people?" he asked.

"Dead people are often more likable than the living." Ava flashed him a superficial smile.

Malcolm scoffed. "Suppose everyone needs some sort of wee hobby."

Wee hobby?

"Actually, I love cemeteries," I said, rather than tossing my expensive Bordeaux in the man's face. "My grandma was a genealogist."

"It was the first place we went when we got here," Biddy added. "Just came from there, oh, fifteen minutes ago."

Panic flashed in the man's blue eyes, yet his smile remained. *Had we seen or heard him and his mistress inside the abandoned church?*

"I must say, the graveyard is better kept than much of the hotel." He eyed his sister. "Out of all the luxury castles in Scotland, why in the world did you select this one?"

Ava's gaze darkened, and Rhona's jaw tightened.

"I love it," I blurted out.

"It's totally brill," Biddy said. "I hate hoity-toity hotels where you're afraid to touch a thing for fear of breaking it and cleaning out your bank account."

As if Biddy and I had ever stayed at a hoity-toity hotel.

Malcolm gave us a tight smile. "I suppose it needed to be a location affordable for all family members."

I bit down on my lower lip. Biddy tensed next to me.

"Going to step out for a fag." Malcolm raised his Scotch

glass and strolled off, his mistress's gaze following him out the door.

I relaxed my teeth against my lower lip before I drew blood.

Rhona recovered with a faint smile. "If you'll excuse me, I'm going to run to the loo and then grab another drink." She smiled sweetly before polishing off her Scotch.

"Would be needing several stiff drinks if I were married to my bloody brother," Ava said.

"Referring to Malcolm, not me, I hope," a man asked, walking up behind Ava. He was dressed in jeans, a navy henley, and a gray wool blazer. His dark hair was graying around the temples, and his dimpled smile included his blue eyes, which eased the tension in the air.

"Of course, pet." Ava gave him a kiss on the cheek. "And you also aren't the reason I'm heading off to the loo the moment you joined us."

"Will try not to be taking it personally."

Dad smiled, shaking the man's hand. "Great to see you. And to see you have great taste in beer." The two men clinked their bottles of the same local craft beer. Cemeteries were on my bucket list, whereas local beers were on Dad's. "Was hoping you'd be here." He introduced Biddy and me to Ian Murray.

"Actually, Mags met me and my two brothers nearly twenty years ago when she was a wee bonnie lassie," Ian said.

Thankfully, I hadn't remembered Malcolm. I did, however, remember Ian, the kind man who'd brought me a souvenir from Scotland and played crazy eights and go fish with me instead of poker with the men. "Sad to say my *Lady Mags Murray* T-shirt no longer fits."

He smiled. "Aye, should have bought ya another."

"Is Tavish here?" Dad asked.

"Nay. Won't be back from Africa for a few days. Is on a monthlong photo shoot for a wildlife magazine."

Rhona returned, and we chatted about things to do in Edinburgh and the nearby quaint village of Dalwade, filled with shops, cafés, and, most importantly, a cemetery on my walking map.

The castle's owner, Archie McLean, an English gent, marched into the room on a mission. The short white-haired man had greeted us upon arrival at the hotel. He was definitely more of an Archie than an Archibald. Like the castle, he was a bit disheveled in a wrinkled blue linen blazer with the Kerr family crest on the right breast, navy slacks, and blue suede loafers. A large man in a dark suit closed the door behind him, and conversations ceased.

"I'm afraid I have some distressing news." Archie's voice cracked, and he patted sweat from his forehead with a white hankie. "There has been a theft. Someone has stolen the Robin Hood arrow."

A collective gasp filled the dungeon.

Archie wiped his face with the hankie. "My sincere apologies, but nobody may leave this room until the police arrive and have had a chance to question everyone."

Panic seized Biddy's face, and her gaze darted around the windowless room, likely searching for the best spot to tunnel her way out. "Janey." She scratched her neck.

We couldn't even take a vacation from a mystery.

At least it wasn't a dead body on my grandparents' graves this time.

Two

FIFTEEN MINUTES later a police officer in a black uniform and a middle-aged plainclothes detective with graying red hair arrived. Biddy's neck was nearly scratched raw, and she'd polished off two Scotches. The last time she'd drunk hard liquor, she'd woken up under a tree in her neighbor's field with two sheep glaring down at her.

"Now I know how prisoners felt locked in here for weeks, surviving on rats until they starved to death." Biddy plucked an ice cube from her glass and swept it over her flaming cheeks.

Dad gave her a sympathetic smile. "No need to worry about starving with a full bar and plenty of rodent-free appetizers. Try the—"

"Open that door now!" Malcolm demanded, getting in the security guard's face. When the man refused, Malcolm's gaze darted to the detective. "You can't be holding me here against my will."

"Aye, we can," the detective said. "Can even be arresting ye for impeding an investigation. Any particular reason ye don't wish to be assisting with solving the crime?"

"Because I don't know a thing about the bloody theft. My suite likely costs more than some old arrow. Why would I nick it?"

Rhona slipped away from her husband, popping a pill into her mouth and washing it down with a Scotch. A short elderly woman with red glasses and lipstick went over and appeared to scold Malcolm for his behavior. Rather than walloping him with her Murray tartan–patterned purse, the woman gestured for him to take a seat at her table. Raking a frustrated hand through his dark hair, Malcolm went over and dropped down in a chair next to the three white-haired women.

"Let's hope he gets himself arrested so we won't have to deal with him the rest of the reunion," Dad said. "He was just as big a jerk when he visited us in Chicago. Talked about nothing but himself the entire time."

"If I were Rhona, I'd hit the bar and act like I didn't know the eejit." Biddy scratched at her neck. "Fancy another drink?"

Dad nodded. "How about I buy you lovely lasses one along with some appetizers?"

"That'd be grand." Biddy handed him her empty glass.

Hopefully, I'd packed earplugs to drown out Biddy's snoring.

The plainclothes detective joined us and introduced himself as Detective Inspector Henderson. Biddy fanned her bright-red cheeks with her black leather clutch.

"Okay, are ye?" he asked Biddy.

She smiled. "Grand, just grand."

"What were your lassies' roles in this evening's event? Waitressing?"

We'd gone from being the evening's entertainment to the waitstaff? I informed him we were guests and supplied our personal information along with Dad's.

"We just saw the arrow a half hour before the owner announced it was stolen," I said. "We didn't notice any suspicious characters skulking around the corridor."

"So far you're the last ones to have seen the arrow. Except for the thief, of course."

"That's fierce bold for someone to have smashed the glass and nicked the yoke right in the open," Biddy said.

The detective arched a curious brow. "How'd ye be knowing the glass was smashed?"

Biddy's fanning increased, and her crimson cheeks burned even brighter. "Ah, er, I'm assuming the display case was smashed. How else would someone have gotten into it unless the person had a key? And then you'd be questioning the staff rather than us."

He nodded. "It wasn't smashed, but everyone is still a suspect. There's a hidden passageway just down from it. The person may have escaped through there without having been seen."

"A secret passage?" Biddy and I muttered in awe.

"It's like Nancy Drew," Biddy said.

I held up a halting hand. "Don't even get started on another Nancy Drew book." *The Mystery of the Person in the Purple Pouch* was the title we'd given to our mystery two months ago, when I'd found a dead man on my grandparents' graves, planning to bury what turned out to be Grandpa's relative's remains in a purple velvet pouch.

"Is that the passageway haunted by Euphemia's ghost?" Biddy asked.

The man shrugged. "Not sure."

"You should find out and add her to your suspect list," she said. "Her ghost has been spotted by dozens of guests over the years."

His gaze narrowed on Biddy, clearly unsure how to respond. That was a fairly common reaction when someone first met her.

"And just because we're staying in Euphemia's Quarters doesn't mean we nicked the arrow because we need the money. We're merely intrigued by its history. The room, not the arrow."

I shot Biddy a look telling her to shut her yap before we were the ones arrested rather than Malcolm for his temper tantrum. As if her nervously scratching her neck raw didn't make her look guilty as it was.

Dad returned with three sparkling waters rather than liquor and small plates overflowing with fancy appetizers. I popped a crab-stuffed mushroom into my mouth.

"Do you recall anything else?" the detective asked.

"That Malcolm fella stepped outside for a fag," Biddy said. "Was gone an awfully long time."

Because he was likely in the cemetery with his mistress. Since his affair likely didn't play a role in the theft, I didn't mention it.

Dad gave the detective the names of everyone we were talking with during the time the theft occurred. "Most stepped away at some point during our conversation except the three of us."

"I also noticed the bartender made a liquor run and

returned within ten minutes," I said.

"You're quite observant," the detective told me.

Biddy nodded. "Mags is a detective. I'm her assistant."

"Stop telling people I'm a detective all the time."

"Well, you are. She's brilliant at finding dead people."

Detective Henderson arched a curious brow.

"I'm a genealogist." I snapped my mouth shut and glanced around, hoping nobody had overheard me disclosing my profession. Ava and Rhona were nearby but didn't appear to have been eavesdropping on our conversation.

Biddy pointed at the man's notepad. "Don't forget to write down that Malcolm fella went outside for a fag. He likely went out back to the garden, so would have passed right by the arrow."

"Yes, I got it," he assured her.

Ava apologized to everyone as we left, ensuring us this was standard procedure and certainly none of the Murrays were strong suspects. That the thief had undoubtedly taken advantage of the empty corridor while the group was tucked away in the dungeon, clueless as to what was happening.

"Remember, we're here on vacation, not to solve a mystery," I told Biddy as we headed up the stone staircase with Dad.

"What if the owner offers a reward that would pay for all of our spa appointments and guest room."

"I don't have any appointments, and my dad paid for our room. We're on vacation."

No daylight through the windows and numerous burned-out chandelier bulbs made the dimly lit stone corridor the ideal spot for a theft. Blue-and-white crime-scene tape roped off the stolen arrow's empty glass case.

Biddy and I peeked behind heavy tapestries and swept a hand along the wall, searching for a loose stone that might open the door to the secret passageway. No luck.

"I'm fine with people knowing you're a genealogist," Dad told me after the last guest passed us by. "You might want to share a few tricks of the trade with Ava. Don't feel you need to hide the fact on my account."

"How would I explain I'm a genealogist yet hadn't traced our Murray tree?"

I'd recently traced Mom's Fitzsimmons line when solving Grandpa's purple pouch mystery. Grandma had already traced her Flanagans back five generations.

"Because you're a busy girl, and I knew I could contact the Murray clan for family history."

We headed up the blue-and-gold carpeted open staircase leading to the guest rooms.

"You need to forgive her, Mags, and let it go," Dad said.

"I will." One day.

How had he so easily forgiven Mom? I would hold grudges to my death. A trait I'd inherited from her. She was responsible in more ways than one for my continued anger. However, I couldn't allow her to cause a rift between Dad and me. I needed to figure out a way to get over it.

When we arrived at the third floor, Dad gave both Biddy and me a kiss good night on the forehead before heading to his William Wallace Suite. The Scottish hero hadn't been a castle guest, having died two hundred years before it was built. It was still cool to have a room named in his memory.

Biddy and I trudged up another three flights of stairs, huffing and puffing by the time we reached the top floor to retire to our servants' quarters for the evening. Upon entering the cheerful yellow room with an exposed stone wall, I nearly stumbled over my suitcase at the foot of the twin bed. I heaved it on top of the bed's green floral quilt, hoping it would fit underneath the bed once emptied. We'd agreed to share the small closet and dresser and to use the third bed for overflow clothes.

Steps led up to the extra bed and chair in a small nook with the room's only windows looking out at the tower's defensive wall obstructing the view. After struggling with the lock, Biddy pushed up the window. A fly flew in on a cool breeze. A shiver crawled over me, yet I didn't complain, not wanting Biddy to have another claustrophobia attack. I'd have to remember to close it before going to bed so I wouldn't wake up in the middle of the night with a bat swooping around the room.

"How unfair that a jerk like Malcolm is staying in the Queen Victoria Suite when good, hardworking people like us are in the servants' quarters," Biddy said.

We weren't exactly slaves to our jobs. Biddy still only worked three days a week as a pediatric nurse, and my genealogy business had slowed. My work would pick up after our live Halloween episode on *Rags to Riches Roadshow*. Especially since I was receiving credit as a cowriter. This past spring Biddy and I had appeared on the show about our role in locating a missing person, Aidan Neil, and his family heirloom—an unpublished manuscript involving a famous Irish author. The upcoming episode would feature my family heirloom—the gold locket, a piece of mourning jewelry, had helped me trace Grandpa Fitzsimmons's mysterious family line and locate living relations. I was excited to share my story despite being nervous about how Biddy and I might screw up during a live filming.

"Staying in a Scottish castle isn't exactly slumming it," I said.

Biddy wore a giddy smile and flopped back on her twin bed. "I know. How awesome is this?" Her gaze narrowed on two small boxes wrapped in blue paper with gold ribbons on the wooden desk. "What are those?"

We tore open the gifts, each containing a purple floral design teacup. According to the card, the cups were a replica of Queen Victoria's china collection.

"A proper cup for tea in the Queen Victoria Suite with Rhona," Biddy said.

I uncorked the bottle of red wine we'd bought at the airport. I poured a splash in each cup, then corked the bottle for the night, since Biddy's near-death experience in the dungeon had sobered her up.

"Let's have a welcome drink on our private veranda." Biddy went up to the bed nook. She swung a leg up over the windowsill and pulled herself up, then crawled out onto the tower. I handed her the teacups before joining her. Stars and twinkling lights from the nearby village of Dalwade illuminated the evening sky. No mooing cows or baaing sheep filled the air. Even the earlier breeze had turned in for the evening.

Biddy and I gently clinked our china cups. "Sláinte."

"To no more drama this trip," I said.

Why did I have the feeling I'd just jinxed us?

Three

THE FOLLOWING MORNING, Biddy and I dragged our butts out of bed a half hour before breakfast ended. Just looking at the corked wine bottle on the desk made my stomach lurch. Thankfully, the reunion's breakfast-bingo icebreaker was tomorrow. It would take an urn of tea before I'd feel sociable enough to mingle and meet people.

We tossed our hair up in ponytails. Biddy exchanged her pj's—Scooby-Doo nurse's scrubs—for a pair of green patterned yoga pants and a purple T-shirt. I stripped off my plaid flannel bottoms and slipped on black yoga pants and a pink T-shirt that read *Dublin Mudslide*. Rather than purchasing the shirt at a Dublin pub, I'd bought it at a Vermont shop I'd worked at one fall. The shop was located near the Flavor Graveyard, where all Ben and Jerry's retired ice cream flavors were laid to rest. Too bad the Irish cream liquor ice cream with chocolate chip cookies had passed on before I'd had a chance to try it.

"No need to worry about being mistaken for staff or

entertainment today." I walked out of our room. "We'll probably get kicked out of breakfast for vagrancy."

We trudged down four flights of stairs to a full Scottish breakfast being served in the music room. It was one of two of the hotel's four restaurants currently open. Painted portraits of former ladies of the estate hung on the light-green walls. The elderly lady in red glasses who'd repri-manded Malcolm at last night's reception was playing a lively tune on the grand piano while her two friends clapped along. The white-haired friend had on a casual pink outfit with a matching walking cane hooked on the back of her chair. The lady with a brown curly wig wore a pant set that looked like it was designed by Picasso, with brightly colored geometric shapes.

Biddy massaged her temples. "I need some aceta-minophen."

"We need some water to rehydrate."

We made a beeline for the beverage station and slammed a glass of cold water. While drinking another glass, we went to check out the photo boards perched on easels along the wall. I'd contributed several family photos, including a black-and-white wedding photo of my great-grandparents. It was their last photo taken in Scotland before they immigrated to the US in the early 1920s. Too bad the photo wasn't in color. My great-grandpa had on a plaid kilt, a matching tartan shawl draped over one shoulder of his velvet blazer, Argyle socks, and black shoes. It would have been quite an elaborate and colorful ensemble for a groom. His wife was wearing a typical long lace wedding dress.

"Look at how cute you were." Biddy pointed out the

photo of the three Murray brothers visiting us in Chicago when I was seven. I wore a bright smile and my Lady Mags Murray T-shirt. My sisters were wearing red plaid wool caps. "Why weren't your sisters wearing T-shirts with Lady Emma and Lady Mia on them?"

"Because they requested berets, as if our cousins were visiting from France. The men improvised."

Desperately needing tea, I selected a yellow floral cup from an eclectic china collection. I filled it with hot water and two tea bags. The buffet resembled a full Irish breakfast, except for a tattie scone (a floppy potato pancake) and Lorne sausage (square pieces of meat). I turned my nose up at the sausage.

I smiled at a basket containing a familiar-looking pastry Grandma Murray used to bake. Butteries. The round pastry resembled a flaky croissant. The name "buttery" made no sense. Grandma had used a ton of lard rather than butter to make them, which had likely made them even tastier. My grandparents' home had always smelled like fresh-baked goods and menthol arthritis ointment. They moved from Chicago to Florida when I was twelve. After they passed away, Dad inherited their condo, where he had been living full time since shortly after Mom's death.

I took two butteries along with jam while Biddy loaded her plate with every hot item on the buffet, making my stomach toss.

No way was I drinking the rest of the trip.

I waved across the room at Rhona, sitting at a corner table with Malcolm. The couple waved back. Rather than sneering, I forced a smile at her obnoxious husband.

We joined Dad at a table overlooking the garden with a

distant view of the cemetery's stone wall. After the archery team-building event, I was grabbing my aluminum foil and escaping the living for a few hours.

Dad's gaze narrowed on my casual ensemble. "Late night?"

I dropped down onto a worn green velvet chair. "Too *early* of a morning."

"Early? You missed an incredible sunrise and invigorating morning run." He glanced over at the staff removing the chafing dishes. "Was about to start making you girls each a plate."

Biddy smiled. "We're grand."

"Remember these?" I asked Dad, holding up a buttery.

"Not quite as good as your grandmother's, but close. When your mother found out how much lard was in the pastry, she'd pitch a fit if I ate more than one." He stared reminiscently at his half-eaten pastry.

"Yeah, she was always looking out for your health." I slathered jam on the flat side of the flaky pastry, like Grandma had taught me was done in Scotland. "I should make these sometime. After baking all the pies with Rosie for the school reunion this summer, a buttery recipe would be a breeze."

My sister Mia, who'd recently dropped ten grand on a double convection oven, had inherited Grandma Murray's recipes. Before I'd inherited Grandma Fitzsimmons's home in Ireland and we were still on speaking terms, Mia was always emailing me recipes I never made. Now I'd have to suck it up and ask her for a copy of Grandma's buttery recipe. Probably best to have Dad contact her for it.

Archie McLean popped by our table, dressed in his signature wrinkled blue logoed blazer, tan slacks, and blue suede loafers. "I do hope you're enjoying your breakfast. I sincerely apologize for the inconvenience last evening, but I fear it was necessary. Nobody was excluded from the police questioning, including the hotel staff as well as myself."

"No worries. We're happy to help in any way we can," Dad said. "I hope you recover the arrow. A nice bit of history."

"Indeed, it's a fine piece of history. Guests come here expecting to see it. A fixture of the castle for centuries goes missing only two years after I inherited the place from a distant cousin." A distressed look wrinkled his brow. "One day Agnes, rest her soul, and I were running a small coffee shop in Yorkshire and the next living in a castle. I have quarters in the west wing, and our resident archer, Garrett Maxwell, and his wife live in a small cottage on the grounds."

"The place is incredible," I assured him. "I promise to leave a raving review on Tripadvisor."

Since graduating from high school, I'd posted over a hundred reviews while traveling the States for my seasonal jobs. I always tried to note something positive. Like when I had to spit an avocado wine back into my glass at a Napa vineyard-slash-avocado farm. *The wine is a lovely shade of green, with a fruity aroma and bursting with nutrients.*

Biddy smiled. "I'll sign up for an account."

Malcolm waltzed over in crisply pressed jeans and a cream cashmere sweater. Biddy's smile faded, my back tensed, and Dad managed a smile hello.

Malcolm flashed his pearly whites. "Breakfast was braw," he told Archie. "However, the tattie was a bit off. I'm sure my wife would be happy to share the Murray family recipe with your chef."

Archie gave him a gracious smile. "I will let him know."

That'd certainly go over well.

"Also there appears to be no hot water in the Prince Albert Suite. If you could please have that taken care of." He offered Archie a twenty-pound bill, which the man politely declined.

"It's my pleasure to have that looked at straightaway. Have you given any further thought to our discussion about your wife's idea?"

"Not yet." Malcolm gave the man a pat on the back. "I'll get back to you on that soon." He sauntered off.

We all breathed a collective sigh of relief he hadn't joined us.

Archie smiled. "He and his wife, Rhona, are considering investing in the hotel. Costs a fortune to run a castle nowadays." The owner went off to check on the hot-water situation.

Biddy glared across the room at Malcolm talking with the three elderly women. "He and Rhona are in the Queen Victoria Suite. Gee, I wonder who's in the Prince Albert Suite."

"How bold, filing your mistress's complaints for her."

"I don't care to know what that's about." Dad set the napkin from his lap on the table. "Have a quick call to make before the archery event."

"Work?" I asked in a disapproving tone.

"I promise to keep it short." He gave me a reassuring wink.

If he didn't show up at the archery course, I'd be knocking on his door. This was his first vacation since Mom's death four years ago. He'd been throwing himself into his work, having just finished a major architectural project in Montreal. No way was I losing my dad to a stress-induced heart attack or stroke.

Biddy managed to polish off every bite on her plate, whereas I wrapped a buttery in a napkin to take back to the room. Archie was standing by the door, wishing guests a lovely day.

"Have you thought about offering a reward for the arrow?" Biddy asked him.

"What a splendid idea."

"Mags and I have been known to solve a few mysteries. Have you heard of Brendan Quigley?"

"Of course," he said.

"We helped recover an unpublished manuscript written by his lover."

Actually, we'd found the manuscript when helping to locate Aidan Neil. His grandma confessed to having swiped it for its own protection. However, we had found Aiden after unwittingly leading a potential kidnapper to him. Despite the person having shot him, I'd earned a good chunk of money for discovering the family's true relationship to the famous author. I'd split it with Biddy. She'd thought she'd won the lottery and cut her hours at work. Home maintenance was whittling away at mine. Biddy had also gotten a boyfriend out of the deal. Collin Neil, Aidan's brother, a guy Biddy had the hots for years ago until she caught him kissing another girl.

"Maybe you saw us on the *Rags to Riches Roadshow* episode we starred in about the manuscript," Biddy said.

Archie's gaze narrowed. "Don't believe so. However, I do on occasion watch the show."

"Well, you can always stream it. We're going to be on a live Halloween episode next month. Can't share what it's about." Biddy leaned in and lowered her voice. "Confidentiality agreement."

Biddy telling the man to stream the show wasn't adhering to her promise to not disclose my profession. The episode discussed my genealogy background.

"But it might have something to do with Mags having had outlaw rellies similar to Robin Hood. Stealing jewels from the English to give to the poor Irish. It's in her blood."

"That would mean *stealing* is in my blood. And actually, it turned out my ancestor likely hadn't stolen the jewels and was framed." I glanced over at Archie. "I didn't steal the arrow."

"I thought not."

Until Biddy put the idea in his head.

She'd also put one in mine.

"I could mention your castle to Kiernan Moffat, one of the show's appraisers. It would make a great filming location."

If the undisclosed venue for the mourning jewelry episode hadn't already been selected, the castle would have been perfect. Castle guest Queen Victoria had made mourning jewelry en vogue by wearing her late husband Albert's photo in a locket for forty years after his death.

Hopefully, it wouldn't be too awkward working again

with the show's appraiser. After discovering Grandpa Fitzsimmons's ancestors' sketchy past, I'd had second thoughts about
appearing on the upcoming episode about them. Kiernan
Moffat had threatened to do the show with or without my
approval. So I'd threatened to turn him in to the authorities
for his involvement in the missing Neil manuscript even
though I couldn't prove my suspicions. For years the dodgy
appraiser had been flying just far enough under the radar to
not have been arrested. In the end, I'd opted to do the show.

Archie clapped his hands together. "That'd be splendid
indeed. The theft might add a bit of intrigue, making the
castle an even more enticing location for the show. Hopefully, the arrow will soon be recovered." He shook his head.
"Strange that the display case's key was still in my desk. Thief
must have picked the lock." He pressed both hands firmly
down the front of his blazer, as if trying to iron out the wrin-
kles. "I best notify staff of the reward. Do you think a thousand pounds would suffice?"

Biddy and I nodded. It would motivate *us* to find it if we
weren't on vacation.

Archie tapped a blue suede shoe against the floor. Chop,
chop. He was off to make reward posters.

"Janey," Biddy muttered. "What's the yoke worth?"

"Doesn't matter, and neither does the reward. We're on
vacation."

"Fine. I can lead this investigation without you. Instead
of playing Watson to your Sherlock Holmes, I can be...In-
spector Clouseau. He solved plenty of mysteries without any
assistance."

The bumbling inspector solved mysteries thanks to sheer
dumb luck. Something Biddy and I often relied on.

After having been mistaken for the entertainment and then waitstaff at last night's reception, I preferred not to wear the outfits we'd brought for the team-building event. However, Biddy had put a lot of time and effort into finding the green velvet caps with an orange feather and matching green tunics. At least I'd talked her out of renting the full Robin Hood costumes.

It was a gorgeous fall day, and we headed down a gently sloping hill to the archery course. Six targets were mounted on the front of round straw bales set on easels. A dozen people were already there practicing, swiftly launching arrows straight into the bull's-eyes. A tall middle-aged man dressed in a blue Under Armor windbreaker and jeans—likely the archer Garrett Maxwell—was assisting the elderly woman in red glasses with assembling her takedown recurve bow. Participants were encouraged to bring their own equipment as long as they used a basic recurve or long bow. No high-tech compound bows permitted so that everyone would be on an even playing field. A good thing I'd taken several lessons over the years when attending the Scottish Highland Games back home.

Malcolm strolled over from his target carrying a hand-crafted recurve bow—a gorgeous piece of maple with an inlaid design. His gaze narrowed on our outfits. "Why are you two dressed like elves? Isn't a costume event, is it?"

Biddy forced a sweet smile. "We aren't elves."

"Peter Pan, then, are you?"

"Rise and rise again until lambs become lions." Biddy quoted the famous line from the movie. She'd sucked me into watching several versions of *Robin Hood* when she learned we were participating in the archery event.

Malcolm still looked clueless.

"Snakes don't walk—they slither," Biddy said.

His gaze darkened.

"Robin Hood," Biddy spat. "You know, the legendary heroic outlaw from English folklore who stole from the rich and gave to the poor."

"Aye, that bloody wally."

He smirked and went over to meet Rhona heading down the hill with Ava, who was carrying a blue bow. Rhona wore dark jeans and a beige sweater. A clip held back her brown hair. The two women gave us a friendly wave.

Biddy smiled and waved. "I hope I shoot *him* with a stray arrow rather than some poor bird."

Malcolm's mistress, Izzy, strutted down the sloping hill dressed in tight black pants, black riding boots, a green plaid wool blazer, and a stylish scarf tied around her neck.

"This is archery, not bloody polo," Biddy said.

I nodded. "The place doesn't even have riding stables."

The woman walked over and immersed us in the scent of bergamot and vanilla. She introduced herself as Isabel Murray. Murray? Not a blood relation to Malcolm, I hoped.

"Could you please tell me which group I'm with?" she said.

"Haven't a clue," Biddy said. "Not even sure which group we're with."

Izzy's perfectly tweezed brows narrowed in confusion, then a glint of realization flickered in her green eyes. "Oh, don't I feel like a muppet. So sorry. Thought you worked here." She smiled. "Cute outfits."

There'd been fifty people max at the reception and she couldn't recall having seen us?

The archer's wife, Charlotte, a short blond woman in a blue windbreaker, was distributing arrow quivers and arm and finger protectors. She gave us our assigned targets.

Biddy's gaze narrowed in concern on the brown leather shooting glove and arm protector. "Why does my arm need protecting?"

"From string slap against your forearm and hand," Charlotte said.

Biddy flinched. "That sounds painful." She slipped her hand into the fingerless leather glove and fiddled with the adjustable cord-laced eyelets.

"Oh, I won't be needing either," Izzy said. "I'm here to watch. Wasn't thinking. Should have waited until after the event to have a manicure."

Biddy admired the woman's long red nails. "I have an appointment for a mani and pedi. Can't wait."

"They have a lovely selection of polish."

Charlotte handed Biddy a quiver containing a half dozen arrows with brown feather-tipped ends.

"Now this is brill." Biddy slung the quiver's leather strap across her front, the arrow container across her back. "I feel like Katniss from *Hunger Games*."

"You ladies have fun." Izzy strutted over to her assigned target with the three elderly women.

Malcolm joined us once again and gave Charlotte a charming smile. "Might you have an extra arm protector? My wife has forgotten hers."

Charlotte tilted her head. "Aye. I'll bring one straightaway."

He winked. "I'd appreciate it."

"My pleasure." She flashed him a flirty smile and was off to take care of his request.

He waltzed back over to his wife.

"That was beyond awkward," I said. "Flirting over an arm protector."

Biddy nodded. "Speaking of awkward, if that Izzy woman's last name is Murray, she must be related by marriage, right? Yet she doesn't appear to be here with a spouse. Her perfume costs like three hundred euros an ounce. My coworker wears it, who apparently makes a lot more than I do."

Or who worked five days a week instead of only three?

Ian and Dad joined us. Thankfully, I wouldn't have to hike up three flights of stairs and beat down Dad's door to make him stop working. Besides the two men sharing the Murray smile and dimple, they were about the same height and weight. Both dressed in jeans and wool sweaters, they could have been brothers rather than second cousins.

Ian smiled at our outfits. "Ah, but remember, faint hearts never won fair lady." He bowed, sweeping a hand through the air.

Biddy grinned. "Fair play to ya. That's one of my favorite lines."

While Ian and Dad chatted about their golf outing the next day, Biddy turned to me. "Need to be taking that fella off our suspect list."

"*We* don't have a suspect list because *we* aren't investigating the theft. Remember?"

"I doubt the person stole it for his arrow collection. More

likely to sell it. There are dodgy dealers and collectors who would buy it without provenance."

We'd encountered several of them when searching for the Brendan Quigley manuscript.

Biddy eyed Garrett Maxwell. "Being a famous archer, I bet that fella would know some interested buyers. Maybe he timed the theft when a group was in house to take the heat off himself."

"That's a good point. What guest would have had time to plan the theft when everyone just arrived in the last day or two? A thief would have needed time to case the joint and figure out the particulars. Like how to access the glass case and escape unseen. It's not as if the person smashed it on impulse and swiped the arrow."

Stop investigating the theft!

"Besides the instructor, maybe we should be looking for people who've stayed here before."

"*You* can be looking for previous guests. I'm not investigating the theft."

Garrett Maxwell walked up and gave Dad, Biddy, and me our long bows. We'd provided the archer with our heights in advance so he could determine the draw weight and length best suited for each of us. Ian had brought his own takedown recurve bow.

"I believe one of you bonnie lassies requested lessons." The archer eyed Biddy fussing with her arm-protector cord, still trying to find a comfortable fit. "I'm guessing that's you?"

Biddy nodded, smiling. He assisted her with the protector and loading the arrow into the bow. He demonstrated the proper stance and bow positioning, and then he launched his arrow toward the target. Bull's-eye.

Biddy raised the bow and curled her fingers around the string. She snapped back from the string and bopped her head from side to side.

"Rest the bow string next to your face," Garrett said, guiding the bow closer toward her body. "Keeping your fingers against the corner of your mouth."

Biddy nodded yet continued to lean back from the bow, as if it were about to attack her. "Have ya a face protector, by chance?"

Garrett smiled. "Ya won't be snapping your face."

Biddy stretched her arms out, extending the bow. Throwing herself off balance, she released the string and launched a wobbly arrow into the air. The arrow speared the ground next to Malcolm's brown shoe. The man's darkened gaze darted from the arrow to Biddy, who was standing there wide eyed. He pulled the arrow from the ground. Rather than hurling it through the air like a javelin at a fearful Biddy, he snapped the arrow in half.

Garrett let out a low growl next to me.

The elderly woman with the red glasses witnessed Malcolm's reaction and marched over to him with a stern look. After she had a few words with the man, he whipped a bill out of his wallet. He headed over to Garrett. The men's dark gazes locked, and Malcolm handed the bill to the archer. Garrett slipped it into his pocket without a word. Malcolm returned to his target and continued practicing as if nothing had happened.

Biddy and I heaved relieved sighs.

Dad and Ian took over instructing Biddy so Garrett

could check in with the others. After several failed attempts, Biddy's arrow flew through the air and speared the straw bale just outside the target. We all clapped, and Biddy pumped a celebratory fist in the air. Her confidence boosted, she quickly loaded another arrow. She released the string and let out a distressed squeal, placing a hand to her chest.

She winced. "The string just snapped me."

"They might have chest protectors," Ian said.

"How about a suit of armor?"

"Don't be in a rush to shoot the arrow," Ian said. "Wait until you are in proper form." He peered over at Malcolm angrily gesturing toward Rhona's arrow, which had landed several feet shy of the target. "I'll be right back." He marched over to the couple. While the two men argued, Rhona fled to the beverage station.

"I could fancy a cider," Biddy said.

We went over and joined Rhona, who was sipping a hot apple cider with a shaky hand.

"My fibromyalgia is flaring up," she said. "Sometimes my arm or hand is too weak to even grip a cup, let alone a bow."

The stress of being married to Malcolm had likely caused her chronic condition. I'd once worked with a woman who suffered from overactive nerve damage. The list of symptoms was endless. Besides widespread pain, she'd be ready for a nap at noon, then unable to sleep at midnight. The poor thing had been a hot mess.

Rhona slipped a small jar from her jacket pocket and massaged an ointment over her forearm. A cool menthol scent once again reminded me of Grandpa Murray.

"You should get a proper massage," Biddy told her.

"I could never drop that much quid on something that lasts merely an hour with nothing to show for it."

Whereas her husband's mistress likely had booked back-to-back appointments her entire stay. What would possess a nice woman like Rhona to stay with such a horrible man if it wasn't to spend his money?

Four

⚬⚬⚬

WHEN BIDDY and I entered the library for afternoon tea, I felt like Robin Hood meets *Downton Abbey*. Most women were wearing dresses and fancy hats, and the two elderly men were in suits. That was apparently what the invite meant by *dress accordingly*. We slipped off our green velvet caps, not having had time to change after the archery event. Our team had come in last place. On the upside, Biddy had hit the target, rather than her breasts, at least a half dozen times. I'd done quite well considering I hadn't shot an arrow in eight years. Rhona had sat out the competition, and Malcolm's team had come in first place. The three elderly women had taken second.

Authors from Edgar Allan Poe to Brendan Quigley and Maeve Binchey filled bookcases that rose from the wooden floor to the yellow ceiling with white crown molding. We said hello to everyone as the hostess led us past groupings of brown wingback leather chairs and couches. Cocktail tables showcased silver teapots and three-tier china dessert stands displaying finger sandwiches and a variety of mini desserts and pastries. The hostess seated us at a window table with a view of the front drive. Biddy and I sat on worn leather chairs next to each other. A waitress set a dessert stand on the table with a list of ten teas to choose from.

"Ah, that's lovely," Biddy said, massaging her breast.

I slapped her hand away from her chest.

The waitress gave us an uneasy smile.

I selected the lavender-citrus tea, and Biddy chose a Moroccan mint blend. The waitress left to get our lovely silver teapots.

"You have got to leave your breast alone," I told Biddy.

"Well excuse me, but it hurts." She snagged a fruit tart from the top plate, and I chose a macaroon. "I don't care if that Malcolm fella is rich. So was Pierce Brosnan in the *Thomas Crown Affair*. He nicked paintings from museum walls for the thrill of it, not because he needed the money. Make sure Malcolm is at the top of our list of suspects."

I was done asking *What list of suspects?*

Ava walked over to our table, a Murray tartan silk scarf tied around her neck. "Did you lassies enjoy the archery event?"

"It was grand," Biddy said. "Shot a bow and arrow for the first time. Did brilliantly."

Except for when she nearly speared Malcolm's foot and snapped her breast with the string.

"Hope you've recovered from last evening's unexpected incident. So sorry for that."

"No worries." I waved off her concern. "Wasn't your fault. Besides, we love a good mystery."

"Aye, which is why I love family history. However, I'm not having much success with tracing my mother's Gibson line prior to eighteen hundred. Having a wee bit of difficulty finding some records on Ancestry.com."

"You should check out ScotlandsPeople," I said. "Ancestry.com's database contains a select number of Scottish records. It isn't comprehensive like Scotland's government site."

Ava quirked a curious brow.

My heart raced. "Ah, my grandma Fitzsimmons was a genealogist. I sometimes helped her out a bit."

Ava smiled. "Thanks for the tip. I might pick your brain for some more ideas."

"Who do you think stole the arrow?" Biddy asked, lowering her voice. "It surely wasn't a family member."

"My money is on the archer, Garrett Maxwell. I mean, who else would know the value of such an item?" Ava went over to a couple just seated at a nearby table.

"I agree." Biddy nodded. "We should check into the archer and see if he was recently denied a raise or is unhappy with his job."

"And how do you plan to do that?" I asked.

Biddy shrugged. "I also need to figure out who has stayed here previously and who desperately needs the money enough to risk going to prison." She slipped a paper from her purse with family members' contact information, which we'd received upon check-in. "Interesting that Izzy Murray isn't on the list."

"Maybe she's big on privacy and doesn't want nosey people stalking her on the internet."

The waitress returned with our tea. I blew on the steaming light-colored beverage, then took a sip. The flavor was heavy on citrus and light on lavender. Interesting.

Biddy Googled one of the addresses on her phone. She let out a low whistle and showed me a stately country home on sprawling acres of land. "Guess who lives there?"

"My brother Malcolm," Ian said, having walked up behind us.

Embarrassed, Biddy clicked her phone, and the screen went dark.

Ian smiled. "Nothing wrong with getting to know the family. That was the Murray family home for three generations. May I join you two lassies?"

"Absolutely," I said.

He slid onto a chair. "I just heard the owner is offering a thousand-pound reward for the return of his arrow. I might do a wee bit of investigating myself."

"Who do you think stole it?" I asked.

He leaned in and lowered his voice. "Euphemia."

"Euphemia?" I glanced around the room, not having yet met the woman.

"Lord Kerr's mistress," he said.

Biddy smiled wide. "Ah, fair play to ya. And that police detective acted like I was mad for suggesting she be a suspect. Maybe she hid it in the secret passageway."

A mysterious glint sparkled in Ian's blue eyes. "Should we see?"

Biddy perched on the edge of her chair. "You know where it's located?"

He nodded. "Archie gave me a tour earlier today."

"I have a massage in a half hour, but we could go after dinner," she told him.

"Are you sure you can handle an underground tunnel?" I asked her.

"I'll be grand. I only panic if I fear there's no way out."

"There are several passageways out." Ian gave her a reassuring smile.

"See. I'll be grand. If you just took a tour of the passageway, is this your first stay at the castle?"

"Aye. I live nearby in Edinburgh. Had to come check on a few things for Ava when she was planning the gathering."

Biddy studied Ian, undoubtedly debating adding him back on her list of suspects.

"What do you do in Edinburgh?" I asked.

"I teach history at the University of Edinburgh."

"Mags loves history, especially if it involves dead people." Biddy laughed. "Well, I suppose most history involves dead people. That's why she's obsessed with graveyards. While she's visiting creepy graveyards in Edinburgh, I'm going to take a tour of all the famous filming locations in the area, like for *Outlander* and *The Avengers*."

"How about filming locations in graveyards?" he said. "I'd be happy to take you both on a tour."

"That'd be brill," Biddy said.

We raised our cups of tea to our personal tour guide and ghost hunter.

After we finished tea, Biddy headed to the spa. I slipped on my tennies, grabbed the roll of aluminum foil, and raced out to the cemetery before it was dark. I flew through the open iron gate and came to a halt upon noticing Rhona kneeling in front of a headstone. Dressed in a tan quilted jacket and jeans, she was tracing a finger across the weathered stone.

I joined her. "Foil works great for reading stones, if you'd like some."

"Thanks. It's Lady Kerr's grave. Such a shame it's quite scratched."

I shook my head in disgust. "Somebody used a wire brush to clean away the moss and lichen. So sad how many stones are damaged by people using harsh tools and cleaning products."

"As sad as that poor woman's life. How horrible having the pressure to produce an heir or you ended up in the dungeon or dying a mysterious death."

"And if you had sons, you had to hide them away so nobody poisoned them before one became king. Or even daughters. Look at Queen Victoria. Her mother made her a prisoner in her own home until she became queen at the age of eighteen. At least according to that Netflix show."

Rhona smiled. "I find history fascinating. Ava wants me to assist her with the family research. Of course, Malcolm thinks it's a waste of time. He wouldn't even agree to take a DNA test to help her out."

He didn't want his illegitimate kids coming out of the woodwork, looking for cash.

"My grandma was a genealogist. I spent a lot of time in cemeteries when I visited her in the summer. She'd find this one fascinating, being right next to the castle."

"There is something so peaceful about the place."

I nodded, peering out over the landscape of graves and Celtic crosses. "My birthday in two weeks will be my first one without my grandma." I let out a shaky breath. "Not that I could ever ditch school to spend a birthday in Ireland with her, but she always mailed a box with my favorite Irish treats.

One year she sent a book with humorous grave epitaphs. *Here lie I, and no wonder I am dead, for the wheel of a wagon went over my head.*"

Rhona laughed.

"I know, right? It's hilarious. However, my mom had a fit. Said it wasn't an appropriate gift for a ten-year-old."

"I think that's lovely you and your grandmother had such a special bond."

"I plan to celebrate my birthday with the same treats. Ginger biscuits are my favorite."

"Those are my daughter Sienna's favorite also. She's at university in Australia. She went to school halfway around the world to have her freedom yet insists I send her monthly care packages from home." Thoughts of her daughter put a smile on her face. "Do you have any other birthday plans?"

"I'm sure I'll celebrate with Biddy. Not like I have a boyfriend. I'll be twenty-seven and no boyfriend."

However, I'd made the decision a few months ago to break things off with Finn O'Brien before our friendship grew into something more. He wasn't emotionally recovered from a near-fatal car crash, and I wasn't emotionally prepared for a guy to infringe on my time with Biddy and my genealogy research. I was already in competition for Biddy's time with her new boyfriend, Collin Neil.

"Would be much worse to rush into a marriage just to be married." Rhona frowned. "When I was your age, I was married with a four-year-old daughter. Became pregnant while at university, and our parents insisted we marry. I would never do that to Sienna." She glanced at her watch. "I best head in. Meeting Ava for a drink. Have a lovely time." She headed off.

As Biddy would have said, I'd best get crackin'. Dusk would be settling in soon, so I decided to stay on fairly even terrain. I headed over to a cluster of small headstones by the stone wall. Several of the more recent stones were legible.

Wordsworth the Bestie Westie. Died 1984.

Enid. Thank you for producing sixteen calves and loads of milk.

Princess Beatrice. Born a cat, lived like a lion.

I smiled at Princess Beatrice's headstone. When Biddy and I were twelve, we'd brought home a stray kitten we'd named Beatrice. Biddy's parents wouldn't let her keep the animal due to her dad's allergies, so Beatrice had lived with my grandma. The pet cemetery would provide more insight into the family's sense of humor and lives than the people buried there. I pulled off a sheet of foil and began documenting generations of pets.

A half hour later, I forced myself to leave while it was still light enough to find my way out of the cemetery. I gathered the sheets of foil and headed out the gate and down the path. As I approached the trellis entrance in the garden's shrub fence, arguing filled the air. I peeked around the tall shrubs. Fuming, Charlotte Maxwell tossed her arms in the air and marched away from her husband and Malcolm. Garrett poked a finger in Malcolm's chest, then stalked off after his wife.

What was that about? Had Garrett caught Malcolm with his wife, or was Garrett just warning him to stay away from her? Or had Malcolm broken more arrows and refused to pay for them?

Was there anyone Malcolm hadn't managed to tick off here in a matter of two days?

Five

BIDDY AND I SKIPPED DINNER, still on a sugar high and full from our afternoon tea treats. We were sitting in blue velvet throne chairs in the back corridor, waiting for Ian to give us a tour of the secret passageway.

Biddy was slouched in the chair, relaxed from her massage, still smelling like the spa's signature lavender-citrus scent. "I hope we have a Euphemia sighting. Or I can at least get a snap of her orb."

"You're sure you're going to be okay in a tunnel without any windows?"

"Stop asking me that. I'll be grand."

Shouting came from the garden. Were Garrett and Malcolm going at it again? Biddy and I sprang from our thrones and flew out the massive wood door. Racing down the dirt path lit by landscaping lights, we skidded to a halt upon encountering Charlotte and Archie standing over Malcolm's body lying on the ground with an arrow in the center of his chest.

"Janey," Biddy muttered.

At least his eyelids were closed, unlike the dead body I'd found on my grandparents' graves. I still had haunting flashbacks of the man's vacant gray eyes staring at me. A shiver crawled up my back, and I glanced away from the body.

"I deserve the reward." Charlotte fumed. "I found the arrow. It just so happened to be in the man's chest."

"You will not be removing the arrow." Archie patted his forehead with a white hankie. "It's quite fragile. You could damage it."

Not to mention they shouldn't be tampering with a dead body and crime scene. The woman didn't seem traumatized from finding a dead man. She already appeared to have recovered.

Garrett raced up, his gaze darting between the body on the ground and his wife. "Are you all right?"

"No, she's not," Archie snapped. "She insists on removing the arrow. I told her she'll do no such thing. It could be damaged if not handled properly."

If shooting the antique arrow through the air at a hundred and fifty miles an hour into the middle of a man's chest hadn't damaged it, I doubted it'd be harmed when being removed. Unless of course, the steel tip had broken off on impact. I cringed at the thought of it.

"What were you doing out here?" Garrett demanded of his wife.

"Was going to the hotel for some chamomile tea. We're out."

Garrett looked skeptical. What had he assumed she was doing out there? Meeting up with Malcolm? Or had he *known* that was what she was doing and killed the man?

Dad and Ian came running into the garden. While I

brought them up to speed, Ian stared in shock at his brother's body lying on the ground.

"Nobody is touching that arrow until the police get here," Dad said.

Charlotte and Archie exchanged glances.

"You have called the police, haven't you?" Dad asked.

"I'll do that straightaway." Archie slipped his phone from his blazer pocket and stepped away.

Izzy strutted up in a pink negligee and matching robe and slippers. Her hair and makeup were still intact. Upon seeing Malcolm on the ground, she let out an earth-shattering scream and dropped onto her knees next to his body. She continued to wail like a banshee, as my grandma would have said.

Dad placed a hand on her arm. "Be careful not to disturb the scene."

Ava walked up and gasped in horror, slapping a hand over her mouth. Survival mode quickly kicked in. "I don't care if that woman wants to make a complete fool of herself, but she won't be making a fool out of Rhona. Get her out of here."

Dad helped a crying Izzy to her feet. Weak in the knees, she collapsed against him for support.

Rhona arrived and stared in confusion at her husband's body. I couldn't even imagine what was going through her mind. Ava slipped an arm around Rhona's shoulder, jarring the woman from her thoughts.

"You couldn't just divorce him, could you?" Izzy spat. "No, that'd have been too easy. You wanted revenge."

"Get her out of here!" Ava yelled.

It took both Dad and Ian to escort Izzy unwillingly back to the castle.

Biddy scratched her neck. "I hope nobody heard me at the archery course saying I'd like to shoot him with an arrow, especially after I almost did."

"I think you proved incapable of hitting the bull's-eye. Besides, we can alibi each other."

"Do you think the killer had planned to use the arrow as a murder weapon when he nicked it? Why use a valuable arrow rather than a cheap one?"

"Maybe the person was sending a message. The Robin Hood arrow was symbolic that Malcolm should have used his money to help others, not merely himself. And that eventually led to his demise."

"I can't imagine Garrett Maxwell would have used the arrow knowing its worth. The archer undoubtedly worshipped such a yoke. He might have had a great motive for stealing it, but what would his motive have been for killing Malcolm?"

"Maybe their argument earlier in the garden had indeed been over Garrett catching Malcolm with his wife. Afraid she was going out to meet him in the garden tonight, he grabbed the closest weapon, which happened to be the stolen arrow he was hiding in his cottage. This seems like a heat-of-the-moment murder rather than a planned one."

Biddy nodded. "Even if Garrett kept his personal bow and arrows in his cottage, he'd have to be an idiot to shoot the man with his own arrow."

"Or brilliant because people wouldn't suspect the most obvious person. And maybe we're the only ones who know Garrett's possible motive."

The three elderly ladies arrived wearing flannel robes and hair curlers. They stood over Malcolm, shaking their heads, their looks saying tsk, tsk, as if scolding Malcolm one last time. By the time Detective Henderson and two uniformed officers arrived, the entire Murray family had congregated near the murder scene. While the officers roped off the area with blue-and-white crime-scene tape, the detective requested that everyone wait inside except for those of us who'd arrived first at the scene.

Garrett slipped an arm around his wife's shoulder, who appeared distraught for the first time since finding Malcolm's body. "This has been a traumatic evening. Can't you be questioning her in the morning?"

"Just a few quick ones for now," the detective said. "However, I'll also need to check the archery course's bows to verify if they're all accounted for."

Garrett nodded. "Of course, but most everyone brought their own equipment. A long bow or recurve one would have been used to shoot an older arrow like that."

"Would imagine it'd be difficult for the killer to sneak in and out of the castle carrying a bow without being seen."

"Most guests brought takedown recurve bows," Garrett said. "One could be disassembled in a matter of minutes or less. The two limbs and a riser could easily be hidden in a bag or even under a coat."

The detective sighed, tapping a pen against his notepad. "Besides everyone having easy access to a weapon, it's not as if ye can verify if a bow was recently used. And people's hands and clothing can't be tested for gunshot residue." He peered back at the body. "A fatal arrow wound is rare. The forensics team has their job cut out for them with this one."

After asking Charlotte a few questions, the detective excused her and sent an officer with Garrett to verify the archery course's bow inventory. Rhona was next on his list to question. Dad and Ian had returned and were helping Ava console the poor woman.

"We were in my room having a spot of tea when we heard the commotion out here," Ava told the detective.

Rhona nodded faintly, still in shock. "I don't know how I am going to break the news to Sienna."

After a few questions, Ava walked Rhona back to her room.

Biddy and I alibied each other, and then I told Detective Henderson about Malcolm and Garrett's argument two hours before he was found dead.

"Did you hear what it was about?" he asked.

I shook my head. "When I came upon them, Charlotte was storming off. I figured maybe Garrett had caught Malcolm flirting with his wife or he was still upset over him breaking an arrow during the archery event. That's merely speculation. Don't quote me on that."

"Well, you can quote me," Biddy said. "Not to speak ill of the dead, but nobody liked the man. I'm not surprised if he'd even alienated the hotel staff. I think a better question would be, who *hadn't* wanted the man dead. Would be easier to try to weed *out* a suspect from the list of fifty people."

Actually, it'd be easier to weed out the Amazon rain forest by hand than to find one person who didn't prefer Malcolm dead.

☘ ☘

A half hour later, the forensics team was on-site, wearing white paperlike jumpsuits over their clothes and hair, blue booties over their shoes, and latex gloves. Detective Henderson was in the process of questioning those people waiting inside. He'd requested we stick around a few days until he questioned everyone more thoroughly and the post-mortem was conducted. At least we were imprisoned in the entire castle and not merely the dungeon.

Dad went to his room, while Biddy and I hung back to talk to Ava. She'd returned from Rhona's room and was sitting on a garden bench by the castle's door on the opposite side of the garden from her brother's body.

"I'm so sorry for your loss," I said.

She peered up, wiping tears from her red blotchy cheeks. "Not much of a loss, I'd say."

Biddy and I exchanged uneasy glances. Not because Ava's candor made us uncomfortable, but because we agreed.

"Sorry." She tightened her Murray tartan–patterned shawl around her shoulders. "I shouldn't be saying such a thing. Even though it's true. You must think me a horrible person."

Biddy and I shook our heads.

"It's just like Malcolm to ruin a family gathering, needing to be the center of attention. After I worked so hard making sure everything was perfect."

I gave her a sympathetic smile. "Don't think he had much control over this situation."

"Aye, one would think it difficult to kill oneself with an arrow, but if there's a way, Malcolm would certainly have found it. He was the most self-centered yet charmed man I've ever known." Her cheeks reddened. "At my tenth birthday party, he was showing off to my friends, who thought he was so cute. He fell and gashed his head. Had to be rushed to the A and E. That was the end of my party. To top it off, all my friends made him get-well cards. My biggest regret in life is having brought Rhona home from university with me that one Christmas. She'd have been best off spending the holidays alone in our hall eating stale vending-machine biscuits and crisps."

The woman's motive for murder was deeply rooted in childhood and guilt over ruining her best friend's life.

"Of course, Rhona would never have left him, for Sienna's sake. What a horrible call for her to have to make. Delivering the news that her father died when she's thousands of miles away in Australia. It'd be different if he'd died in an auto accident or from natural causes. But murder... Would have been easier if Malcolm *had* abandoned the poor lassie."

"Abandoned Sienna?" I asked.

"Rhona was three when her parents divorced. She never saw her father again. She felt if she and Malcolm divorced, he'd have made little effort to have a relationship with their daughter. He'd have moved with Izzy to the South of France, never to be seen again." Her body trembled with anger.

"Rhona knew about Izzy?"

Ava shook her head. "Nay. Not until that daftie insisted on making a scene in front of everyone tonight. And then she had the nerve to accuse Rhona. At least now Rhona gets everything, not just half like if they'd divorced. Not that she killed him for that reason. She couldn't hurt anyone, no matter how much the person hurt her. I'd have killed him before she ever would have."

"You might not want to mention that when you talk to the detective in the morning," Biddy said.

"I won't be telling the police a bloody thing. I'm not about to be responsible for putting some beloved relative away in prison for life."

"Maybe the killer isn't a relative," I said.

The woman shrugged, apparently not wanting *anyone* to go to prison for ridding the world of her brother. "Thankfully, Rhona and I are able to alibi each other. We were in her suite enjoying a Scotch."

Ava had told the detective they'd been in *her* suite enjoying a spot of *tea*. Maybe they'd been having a spot of Scotch with their tea in one of the rooms. Either way, it still seemed odd that they hadn't arrived at the scene together, having supposedly been hanging out with each other.

"Suppose I should offer to plan the funeral," Ava said. "Rhona won't be up to it. Being the only woman in the family, I'm always expected to plan everything."

Including her brother's murder?

Biddy and I left Ava to grieve...her spoiled event more so than Malcolm.

"This is a perfect example of how a nasty person like Malcolm would have benefited from my brill idea for a company, Fake Your Wake. When only four people showed up at his wake, he'd have realized everyone hated him. That might have motivated him to become a better person."

"How couldn't he have known everyone hated him? A lot of people didn't hide the fact."

"Because a self-centered narcissist has a high opinion of himself, which he believes everyone shares."

I nodded. "True. If there was hope for Gretta Lynch,

there might have been hope for Malcolm. Yet even Gretta wasn't as nasty as that man." Despite her having nearly killed Finn O'Brien when she'd accidentally run him off the road almost a year ago. And eighteen years before that, she'd nearly killed Biddy and me for uprooting her daffodils. We were now on friendlier terms with the woman, thanks to her assisting us with solving a few recent mysteries in the Ballycaffey area.

We arrived back at our room to find a bottle of Scotch with a customized Clan Murray label. A nice souvenir to display since Biddy had sworn off hard liquor and I never drank it. We tore open two large envelopes with one of our names on each of them. Mine contained a folder with a photo ID and a parchment paper certificate that read *Lady Margaret Murray of Glencoe.*

Biddy let out an excited squeal and held up her Lady Bridget McCarthy certificate. "This says we own a three-meter-by-three-meter plot of land at Glencoe Wood, wherever that is."

"Who cares where it's at. It's in Scotland!"

According to the pamphlet, the organization sold ten-foot-by-ten-foot plots of land to fund a nature preserve. Scottish landowners, known as lairds, were called lords in English, the female equivalent being ladies. Biddy and I were now titled land gentry.

I opened the small card with the envelopes confirming the gifts were from Ava, Ian, and their brother Tavish, who was currently in Africa. *Since you've outgrown the T-shirt, we thought we'd buy you a gift you could never outgrow.*

"Do you think Malcolm preferred not to be included in the gift, or wasn't asked?" I said.

"Or somebody knew he wouldn't be around for us to thank for the gift. Lady Margaret Murray, would you fancy a glass of wine on the veranda?"

"Yes, I would. Thank you, Lady Bridget McCarthy."

Biddy crawled out the window and onto the tower. I handed her the corked wine bottle from last night and our Queen Victoria teacups. I joined her, and we drank to our new titles.

In the garden below, the forensic teams' bright lights lit the crime scene at the back corner. "Doesn't seem right to be celebrating after what happened tonight. Even if we didn't like the man and barely knew him."

Biddy nodded. "Just think. If we'd been out here earlier, we might have witnessed the murder."

This was one mystery I didn't care to solve. If I was responsible for sending a Murray family member to prison, I'd be the black sheep of the family. Being a skeleton in the closet was bad enough.

Six

THE FOLLOWING MORNING, sunshine and lively chatter filled the music room. Not that I'd expected grieving relatives to be sheathed in black, the elderly pianist to be playing a somber tune while the other women wailed uncontrollably. Yet the atmosphere was a bit lighter than I'd expected. Malcolm was gone, and so was the tension in the air. The only difference from breakfast yesterday was the buffet offered cheesy butteries instead of plain ones. Even the baked goods seemed more festive.

Biddy and I whisked through the buffet. No hangover, I piled a stack of tattie scones on my plate, along with rashers. We joined Dad and Ian at a window table, where the tone was more solemn than the rest of the room. We paid our condolences once again.

"I hate to admit I'm not shocked by what happened." Ian's tired eyes stared into his espresso cup. "With my brother's anger issues, I always figured he'd be the victim of road rage or some poor, verbally abused waiter would lace his haggis with arsenic. Would never have imagined an arrow to the chest." He shook his head. "Thankful that our mother isn't still alive to grieve the loss of a child." He polished off his espresso. "I was sorry to learn about *your* mother passing. Wish I could have made it over for the funeral. Was a lovely person."

I nodded. "Thanks."

Despite our differences and her having had an affair, overall she'd been a good mother. I had to keep reminding myself of fond memories if I was going to be able to forgive her as I'd promised Dad. Like how every birthday she used to make me waffles for breakfast topped with melted Nutella chocolate and bananas. My stomach growled. I added waffles to this year's birthday celebration.

A tall, ruggedly handsome man with thick salt-and-pepper hair and dressed in jeans, a cream wool sweater, and brown hiking boots entered the room. He spotted Ian and headed toward our table, greeting several people along the way. His tanned skin made everyone in the room look even paler.

Ian stood and shook the man's hand. "See you got my message."

The man quirked an eyebrow slashed by a thick scar. "About the noon tee time?"

Dad and I exchanged uneasy glances.

"Sorry. A wee bit too soon for an unsavory joke," the guy said. "But pretending to grieve would make me look guilty of my brother's murder. It's no secret we despised each other." He introduced himself as Tavish Murray, brother number three.

Dad hesitated before shaking his cousin's hand with a gauze-wrapped finger. "What happened?"

Tavish held up an injured hand with several scars and scratches. "Attacked by a lion while I was photographing the herd."

Biddy and I gasped in horror.

"Janey," Biddy muttered.

Tavish wore a sly grin. "Merely joking. But sounds much more impressive than admitting I sliced it on a lid when opening a bloody can of nuts."

"Those tops can be wicked," Biddy said.

We were discussing the risk of opening tin cans when the man's brother had been killed with a steel-tipped arrow.

"You should make up a story about your eyebrow," Biddy told me. "Like you grabbed an antique sword off the castle wall and fought off a thief whose sword tip sliced your eyebrow."

Sounded more heroic than having singed a sliver of my brow off while parading a baked Alaska through a cruise ship's dining room.

"It's a shame it's taken us so long to make it to Scotland," Dad said. "Will definitely change that in the future." He gave me a wink.

I smiled. "Absolutely."

"Even though I'm not a Murray or Scottish, it's a lovely country," Biddy said. "Oh, and I'm now a landowner here."

We thanked Ian and Tavish for their wonderful gift and filled Dad in on it.

Izzy entered the room dressed in a wrinkled purple yoga outfit that looked like she'd slept in it rather than her negligee. Her auburn hair was tossed up in a clip, and her makeup-free skin was blotchy and freckled.

Tavish rolled his eyes. "Jeez."

The woman's green-eyed gaze narrowed on Tavish. Her injection-filled top lip curled into a sneer, and she marched over to the man. "What are you doing here?"

He smiled. "Have a noon tee time."

She slapped the smile off his face, and a red nail flew into the air. She glared at her broken nail. "I just had a manicure."

Tavish massaged his crimson cheek. "I really must stop using that line. Yet I shouldn't have to explain my presence at *my* family reunion, not *yours*, pet. That's the purpose of a divorce."

Izzy was Tavish's ex-wife?

The plot thickened.

"You could at least have the decency to pretend to mourn." Izzy spun around and stalked to the beverage station.

Peering across the room at his ex-wife, a smile curled the corners of Tavish's mouth. He rubbed the indentation on his ring finger, where a wedding band was once worn.

"She's right," Ian said. "If for no other reason, we should be mourning out of respect for Rhona and Sienna."

"Right enough." Tavish pulled a chair over from a nearby table and slid onto it. "Sorry for being such a sod. A bit jet-lagged after a thirty-hour journey."

"Thirty hours from Kenya to Glasgow?" Ian said.

"Got stuck in the Frankfurt airport and spent the night there. Just landed three hours ago. Going on Red Bull. Definitely in need of sleep."

"Aye, you're looking a bit peely-wally."

"Feeling a bit peely-wally." He eyed Ian. "Mind if I crash in your room?"

Ian smiled. "Just like old times. My room has a couch with a pull-out bed."

"Ian mentioned you were on a monthlong photo shoot," Dad said.

"Finishing up a contract job for a wildlife magazine."

"How exciting," I said. "Can't imagine traveling to Africa. I worked at the Milwaukee Zoo one summer selling slushies at the Monkey Island food stand. About the closest I've been to exotic animals."

"Well, we best change that, eh?" Tavish said. "You lassies must pay me a visit sometime. My backyard is like wild kingdom."

"Tavish lives in the Northern Highlands," Ian said. "Leads a bit of a rustic existence, much like our ancestors did."

"I'm about two hours north of your new property. Can be taking you there for a wee visit."

"Our property is in the Highlands?" Biddy said. "Is it near where they filmed *Outlander*?"

"Aye. Not far. We can sleep under the stars and view the northern lights without the city pollution ruining the view. Like in Edinburgh." He smirked at Ian.

"Hey, I don't even own a vehicle."

"Northern Scotland lies at the same latitude as Stavanger, Norway. You have a great chance of seeing the 'Mirrie Dancers.'"

"Merry dancers—how fun," Biddy said. "Is it an outdoor performance with the northern lights in the background?"

Tavish chuckled. "Nay. Mirrie Dancers is what those in the north and on Shetland call the colorful shimmering lights that look like dancers fluttering around the sky.

There is an old Scottish legend that says, when the Mirrie Dancers play, they are likely to slay. It refers to battles among sky warriors or fallen angels, and the blood from the wounded fell to earth and spotted the bloodstones in the Hebrides."

Biddy's nose crinkled. "I like the dancers fluttering idea better. I love sleeping under the stars."

Biddy had never camped in her life. And the last time she'd slept under the stars was when she'd woken up hungover in her neighbor's sheep field.

"What are you lassies up to today?" Ian asked.

"Was thinking maybe I'd play a tune on the pianoforte while Lady Margaret embroideries or weaves her ribbons next to the fireplace. Then take afternoon tea in the library."

I smiled. "We've seen *Pride and Prejudice* a dozen times. We thought about going into the polluted city of Edinburgh but didn't get much sleep, so not sure we have the energy. We're staying on a few extra days in Edinburgh anyway. Think we'll hang out here. Visit the cemetery."

"Or the spa," Biddy said.

"We'll have to do the secret passageway tour tomorrow," Ian said.

I nodded. "We promise not to do it without you."

Ian glanced at his watch, then over at Dad. "The car is collecting us in an hour. I best change."

"Sounds like a good idea. I'll do the same. Told the detective I'd be available for questioning before heading out."

"Aye. Yet if he doesn't catch us, Archie can tell him where to find us. A tee time is nearly impossible for Saint Andrews Old Course between the televised golf events and private ones. Luckily, my mate is an instructor there."

"I might need a few lessons," Dad said. "Been a while since I've golfed."

"Or since he's taken a day off," I said. "Despite living in Florida, where he could golf year around."

"Promise I'll force him to relax," Ian said.

Dad smiled. "And I promise to relax."

Rhona entered the room. A purple-and-green scarf around her neck brightened her drab tan sweater. She wore light-pink lipstick and her brown hair pulled back in a fashionable twist.

It was like Rhona and Izzy had switched bodies overnight.

A sparkle lit Ian's blue eyes, and he locked gazes with Rhona. She smiled at him while we all seemed to vanish into the background. It was like a scene from a romance movie, when a couple was so in love everything around them ceased to exist except for each other.

Were Ian and Rhona in love?

Was that why he was so angry over the way Malcolm had treated Rhona at the archery event—not merely because he was a stand-up guy, opposite of his brother? Had he wanted his brother dead and out of the way? This family had more drama than an episode of the soap opera *EastEnders*.

Tavish went over and embraced Rhona in a big hug.

"I best go check on her," Ian said, standing. "Have a braw day, whatever you lassies decide to do."

Dad stood. "Yes, you lassies enjoy your day, and stay out of trouble."

"What trouble could we get into hanging out at a castle?"

A castle where a murder had taken place twelve hours ago.

"If you see any William and Kate souvenirs, pick us up one, please," I said. "You know the royal couple met while attending college at Saint Andrews."

"Would you girls like to tag along and check out the university and city?"

"Thanks, but I really want to spend some time in the cemetery and maybe even the one in Dalwade."

Dad headed back to his guest room for a quick shower and to prepare for his golf outing so he'd be ready to hit the road after speaking to the detective.

I peered over at Ian and Tavish chatting with Rhona. "Do you think Ian and Rhona are having an affair?"

"If not, they should be," Biddy said.

"I can't imagine he'd have killed his brother over an affair. He's way too nice."

Biddy shook her head adamantly. "No way. Let's forget what we just saw and about his argument with Malcolm hours before he was killed. I'd rather be ignorant than provide the police with incriminating evidence against the man. We need to wait at the entrance for Detective Henderson so we're the first ones questioned. Before we learn anything else that might implicate one of your lovely rellies."

I agreed. This was one mystery I didn't care to solve, but I also wasn't about to withhold information. I'd merely have to be careful how I worded my answers.

Archie was standing by the doorway chatting with Ava, who was dressed in a blue running outfit, with windblown hair and cheeks. Nothing appeared to cure the loss of your brother like a brisk morning run. Ava greeted us with a bright smile. We thanked her for the wonderful gift.

"How long of a train ride do you think it'd be to visit our new land?" I asked.

She shrugged. "Several hours one way, I'm afraid. But lovely countryside."

Biddy frowned. "Suppose we'd be getting a bit of a late start, especially by the time we figured out the train schedule and got ourselves together."

The short elderly woman in red glasses walked over from her table. "When will bingo be starting?" she asked Ava.

Breakfast bingo. I'd completely forgotten about it.

Ava frowned. "Sorry, Auntie Fenella. I decided not to do it. Wasn't sure everyone would be up for it."

The woman's brow knitted. "Whyever not?"

"With the passing of my brother, it was a long night for some."

The woman placed a comforting hand on Ava's arm. "Oh, of course, pet. I understand. Tomorrow, then?"

Ava smiled. "Definitely. Tell your sisters I'm sorry."

The woman gave Ava's arm a pat. She headed back to her table to break the distressing news about bingo having been canceled.

"I'm off for a massage," Ava said. "Just came for a cuppa." She peered over at Archie. "If the detective is looking for me, he can find me in the spa." She spotted Tavish across the room and whisked over to tell him a quick hello.

Nobody appeared overly concerned about making themselves available for questioning to assist in solving Malcolm's murder.

"I'm glad you recovered your arrow, even though it was under such horrible circumstances," I told Archie.

Concern narrowed the man's white eyebrows. "Detective

Henderson assured me every effort will be made to return the arrow undamaged."

"I'm sure no longer having Malcolm to invest in the hotel is a bit disappointing," Biddy said.

"Malcolm had decided to invest, and Rhona is still interested. She understands the hotel's need for upgrades more than ever. Had we the funds to replace the outdoor security system, her husband's murder would have been caught on film. As would have the theft."

I wasn't feeling too secure here right about now.

And how convenient for the thief and killer that the updated system hadn't yet been installed. Had Rhona realized this prior to the theft and her husband's murder? As a possible investor, Archie might have filled her in on the hotel's needed refurbishments.

"Was actually just discussing a few ideas with Ava for expanding the event side of the castle's business." Archie was giddy with enthusiasm. "To promote the castle as a family-reunion venue for surnames that originated in the Edinburgh area. Ava is quite into family history."

"Mags here is—"

"Happy to assist if they need help." I shot Biddy a cautioning look for almost outing me as a genealogist.

"Splendid." Archie clapped his hands together. "Maybe you could pass the word along to Murrays in Ireland."

I would if I knew any there. Besides, would a Murray having been murdered here be an incentive for other Murrays to book the place for family reunions?

"I'd love to be involved with the cemetery restoration if it's in your plans," I said. "My grandma was a genealogist. I was practically raised in cemeteries. I helped her with several restoration projects."

"That'd be lovely if you could lead such a project."

Lead it?

"A shame that it has become rather run down."

Biddy gave me a pat on the back. "Mags will whip it into shape. Her nicknames aren't Tombstone Terminator and Keeper of the Crypt for nothing. However, I guess she'd be fixing rather than terminating tombstones. Anyway, she was given those nicknames after discovering a dead man on her grandparents' graves."

"It's a long story," I told Archie.

He smiled. "Somehow I think you two lovely ladies have quite a few entertaining stories."

Entertaining, embarrassing, excruciating...

Despite apprehension over leading such an important project, I left with a bounce in my step and a slew of ideas in my head. We walked toward the entrance to wait for Detective Henderson.

"Archie had no motive to kill Malcolm, since he'd likely have been the hotel's biggest investor," I said.

"Unless he got to thinking that a murder here might make the place an even bigger draw for shows like *Rags to Riches Roadshow*."

"I can't see him pulling off a murder. And I'm starting to wonder about Garrett Maxwell having killed Malcolm because he'd hit on his wife. Seems a bit drastic and a rather thin motive. So then he also couldn't have stolen the arrow."

"People have killed for less. Like the woman in Sligo who whacked her husband over the head with an iron skillet because he complained his eggs were too runny. The media made her out to be some crazy woman, when that was likely the thing that finally pushed her over the edge. Maybe he'd complained about her cooking their entire marriage and made her feel as if she couldn't do anything right. Proved him wrong in the end. Her aim with a frying pan was spot on."

Just like the killer's aim with the arrow.

"Had something happened to push Rhona over the edge right before Malcolm was killed? After years of living with the nasty man, had she finally snapped? Or had she been patiently waiting for the opportune moment, such as having fifty suspects all in one place?"

"If you solve this murder, the family will never speak to you again for sending a loved one to prison. Even worse, ya might be finding yourself with an arrow in the middle of your chest. Merely being snapped in the chest with the string is painful enough." Biddy winced, placing a hand to her chest.

If I solved Malcolm's murder, even the suit of armor in the back corridor couldn't protect me from angry family members.

Seven

ON THE WAY to the front entrance, we passed by the hotel's registration. Lily, a blond girl who'd checked us in, was sitting behind the antique desk. She wore a crisp blue pantsuit and a perky smile, ignoring the hotel's ringing phone on her desk. Several crumpled pink message notes were next to the phone, and stacks of boxes sat alongside the desk. Lily picked up the phone's receiver and slammed it down as Biddy and I continued toward the entrance.

"Guess she's tired of taking messages," Biddy said.

"Everyone from the newspaper to her grandma is probably calling for the inside scoop on the murder."

Before plopping down onto a blue velvet high-back chair in the small lobby, I studied a brown stain on the seat. Deciding it wasn't fresh, I sat in the chair next to the sweeping staircase leading up to the guest rooms. Biddy sat in a matching chair next to me. A crisp fall breeze blew in through the open front door along with the sound of gravel crunching under the tires of a small gray car cruising up the tree-lined drive. The same as in Ireland, open doors and windows helped prevent mold and musty smells. Keeping my home aired out was easy compared to a five-hundred-year-old castle. Thankfully, my friends Edmond and Rosie were popping by to check in on my house in Ballycaffey. They were also giving Pinky his daily treat, Froot Loops. The neighbor's sheep spent more time in my yard than in his field. Pinky had recently helped me overcome my fear of sheep and was the closest thing I'd had to a pet in years.

"Okay, let's prepare for the detective's questioning," I said. "Ava hating her brother isn't a crime, or everyone would be guilty of his murder. Nothing she said last night would make her a murderer. Who doesn't have childhood memories of sibling rivalry?" Yet I couldn't imagine talking so nasty about my sisters right after one of them was murdered. "And she and Rhona had an alibi. Even if it is a bit iffy."

"For all we know, Ian and Malcolm might have been arguing over an arrow at the archery event." The registration phone rang once again, and rang, and rang. Biddy's gaze darted through the doorway toward Lily. "Can't focus with that constant ringing."

"Well, try. Our theory that Ian loves Rhona is purely speculation. We haven't any solid proof and shouldn't be spreading rumors. We should only tell the detective the facts as we know them."

"Like Malcolm and Izzy shagging in the church that first day." Biddy's top lip curled back. "Rhona hadn't caught them, and according to Ava, Rhona hadn't known about the affair."

"I think that's a bunch of hooey, as my grandma Murray would say. I can't imagine Rhona not having known. But again, that's purely my opinion."

A young brown-haired guy in jeans and a blue jacket, carrying a stack of pink boxes, entered the hotel. Two matching pink bags hung from his forearm by satin ribbons. The packages' black embossed logo read *Chloe's*. He continued through to the reception desk as the phone once again started ringing. Lily let out a frustrated scream, and the ringing stopped. We glanced through the doorway at the flustered receptionist holding the phone cord she'd just yanked from the socket. The poor delivery guy's panicked gaze darted to Biddy and me. We flew over and came to his rescue. He set the boxes on the floor next to the desk and fled. We led the frazzled girl over to a sitting area across from the desk.

"Sorry." Lily plopped onto a blue velvet chair. "The bloody phone won't stop ringing. Reporters and nosey people wanting details on the murder. That lad Alec has been delivering packages nonstop for the Prince Albert Suite. Charlie, the porter, quit after he heard what happened here last night. The guest picked up one package earlier but left the rest."

"If that woman wants her packages, she can bloody well come down and get them," Biddy said.

Lily shook her head vigorously. "It's against policy to be having guests picking up their own packages. But I can't do everything around here. The girl who worked last night was so upset she needed to take the week off." She let out a distressed squeak.

"We'll take care of delivering them after we speak with the detective." I ignored Biddy's disapproving glare, not wanting one more hotel staff to quit on top of everything else going on.

Lily took a calming breath. "Suppose I best be getting

myself together before the detective arrives. Sorry about that. I'm sure Alec thinks I'm an absolute gobshite the way I acted. Just never known anyone who was murdered." She shot us a nervous glance. "Not that I knew the man well or anything, just never have known *anyone* murdered before." Lily popped up from the chair and went back to her desk, plastering on a perky smile.

Biddy and I exchanged curious glances.

"What was that about?" Biddy said as we returned to the lobby. "You don't think something was going on between her and Malcolm, do you?" Her nose crinkled in disgust.

"Despite having been twice her age, I could see him having made a move on her and she'd shot him down." I winced. "Poor choice of words. Or maybe she's just freaked out over someone getting murdered where she works. Can't blame her."

"I wonder if Izzy went on the shopping spree before or after Malcolm's death. A bit of comfort shopping?"

"Can't imagine the boutique would have been open early enough this morning for her to have made such a haul."

We no sooner sat back in the lobby and Detective Henderson strolled through the door with a steaming beverage in a to-go cup. We sprang from our chairs.

He came to an abrupt halt, nearly dropping his cup. "Ah, great to see ye both."

"We're available for questioning, if you'd like," I said.

"Aye. Let's step into the room set aside for me today." He led us to a boardroom with a long wood table surrounded by a dozen wooden chairs with gold padded seats. "How did you two lassies know the victim?"

"He was my dad's second cousin. Their grandfathers were brothers. We hadn't seen him in twenty years."

The detective quirked a brow. "Why'd you choose now to visit after all this time?"

My hands started to sweat. "It's the first reunion they've held, that we know of."

"Did ye bring your own bow?" he asked.

"No. I don't own one. The last time I shot an arrow was at the Scottish Highland Games in Illinois, like eight years ago."

He eyed Biddy.

"I just shot my first arrow yesterday at the archery competition." She smiled proudly. "Did quite well, if I say so myself. Even hit the target a few times." Her smile faded. "I'm not good enough to have shot the man in the middle of the chest. With enough practice I might be. Not that I'd ever shoot a person, even if I could."

I glared at Biddy.

She bit down on her lower lip.

"No bow was missing from the archery course's inventory?" I asked.

He shook his head. "Doesn't mean one wasn't used and returned unnoticed."

"Apparently no prints were found on the arrow either, or you wouldn't still be questioning everyone."

Rather than confirming my suspicion, the detective took a drink of coffee. I recounted our knowledge of what had gone on over the past few days as Biddy and I'd rehearsed.

"You saw, or rather *heard*, the two of 'em in the church that night before the reception?" he asked.

I nodded. "Rhona was calling out to him from the garden but never saw a thing."

Biddy shook her head. "She hadn't a clue about the affair."

That seemed to be everyone's story, and we were sticking to it, not knowing any differently.

"Sure about that?" he asked. "The woman was that oblivious to her husband's philandering despite him doing a pretty shoddy job of hiding it?"

We nodded.

"How did Izzy Murray react when seeing the body?"

"She was a total wreck." Unlike the rest of the family.

Biddy shot me a disapproving glance for pointing a finger away from Izzy and at Rhona.

"As I mentioned last night, the last time I saw the victim, he was arguing with the Maxwells in the garden. No clue what it was about."

I pointed the finger back at Izzy having a motive that she might have discovered she wasn't the man's only mistress.

"So far that puts you as one of the last people having seen him alive." He jotted this fact down on his notepad.

And now the finger was pointed at *me*?

"I hate to speak ill of the dead," I said. "But Malcolm Murray had serious anger-management issues, as I'm sure you realized after the theft. Like Biddy said last night, you're going to be best off trying to find someone who *didn't* want the man dead than trying to determine who *did*."

"Including you two lassies?"

Biddy did an eye roll. "If I'd be risking life in prison for killing someone, it'd have been Collin Neil after catching him kissing that wicked Aisling Donnell. Had the urge to run him down several times when coming across him out walking on the road, but I didn't. Turned out to be a good thing since we're now dating and things are grand." Biddy's dreamy expression faded, her gaze narrowed on the detective's notepad. "Don't be writing that down. Should we break up and he turns up dead, it wouldn't be looking good for me having said that, would it?"

The officer gave Biddy a disturbed look rather than professional advice. And that was the end of our questioning. Biddy had a way of putting people at a loss for words.

I called Dad and told him Detective Henderson was available in the boardroom to question him before his golf outing. Biddy and I headed to the registration desk. Lily was hesitant to violate hotel policy by allowing us to deliver Izzy's packages. I assured her we were great friends with the woman. We were all one big happy family. Except that Izzy wasn't actually part of the family and one member might have killed Malcolm.

Lily loaded us up with packages.

Running out of steam after two flights of stairs, Biddy and I rested a moment on the third-floor landing.

"What if Izzy *had* seen Malcolm and Charlotte flirting and realized he was hooking up with another woman and she wasn't his only mistress?" Biddy said. "Maybe that's what she was distraught over more so than his death. All the time she'd wasted on the eejit."

I shrugged. "Who knows, but she seriously seems to be the only one broken up over the man's death."

"Yeah, she just lost her sugar daddy."

"It sounds crazy, but I think she really loved the jerk."

We all knew what it was like to make a bad choice in men. I'd made several, including my ex-fiancé, Josh, who'd hopped a plane to New Zealand after breaking off our twenty-four-hour engagement.

We arrived at Izzy's suite, and loud crying carried out through the solid wood door and into the hallway.

"Maybe we should come back later," I said.

"If we return these deliveries to the desk, Lily will quit." Biddy rapped on the door.

The crying stopped. A few moments later, Izzy appeared wrapped in a white fluffy spa robe. White flip-flops showed off her red toenails and freshly buffed and exfoliated feet. Her crying jag had left her green eyes red rimmed and puffy. However, her face lit up at the sight of the packages in our arms. She ushered us into the large room with honey-colored walls, a four-poster canopy bed, and green furnishings.

An open champagne bottle in a silver bucket and two crystal flutes sat on a room-service cart. If Izzy had been celebrating Malcolm's death or the success of her murder plot, then why *two* glasses? Considering she'd showed up to the murder scene in a negligee made me think the champagne had been for an intimate night with Malcolm. At what point had things possibly gone south?

"It's so sweet of you to deliver my packages."

We set the boxes and bags next to several other Chloe's packages on a bench at the end of the bed.

"You both have been so nice to me compared to the others."

That wouldn't take much, even though we'd only had a

two-minute conversation at the archery event when she'd mistaken us for staff.

Izzy sat on a green upholstered couch with gold pillows, and we sat on the matching love seat across from her.

"Malcolm was leaving his wife." Reaching for a tissue, Izzy discovered an empty box and burst into tears.

Biddy rushed to the bathroom for tissues while I sat there unsure whether to console the woman. A bit of a moral dilemma. I felt bad for her being the only person who seemed to have truly cared for Malcolm, yet she'd been having an affair with a married man. Biddy returned with a box of tissues.

Izzy blew her nose and got her crying fit under control. "He was finally leaving her." She peered over at the room-service cart. "He proposed last night an hour"—she choked back a sob—"before...he was found." She held out her hand. A diamond surrounded by emeralds sparkled on her left ring finger.

The snake had proposed while he was still married?

Izzy wouldn't have murdered Malcolm when she'd finally gotten her man and his money. Yet Rhona might have. What if Malcolm had asked his wife for a divorce and had confessed he was on his way down a flight of stairs to propose to his mistress?

"It cost nearly seven thousand pounds." She admired the ring. "It's not like I peeked at our credit card account. Malcolm told me."

Their account, which was undoubtedly only in Malcolm's name. Meaning Rhona was responsible for paying off the debt her husband had incurred becoming engaged to his mistress. Talk about a motive for murder. *I'd* have wanted to kill the jerk.

"We were going to elope to Italy in the spring. He knows...or rather *knew*"—her voice cracked—"how much I adore Tuscany. He'd already picked out the location. We planned to spend our honeymoon looking at villas. His wedding present to me. Making my dream of living in Italy come true." She handed me a piece of paper from the cocktail table, with color photos of a beautiful stone villa surrounded by rolling vineyards.

"Ah, that's lovely, isn't it now?" Biddy smiled. "I really must visit Italy."

"He was such a romantic and not a bad guy, like you might have thought. He was just so unhappy in his marriage." She sniffled. "But I'd have made him happy." The tears started flowing once again.

I wanted to ask the woman if she'd planned to be as forgiving as Rhona had been for the past twenty-odd years when Malcolm had likely fooled around on her. Since right after they'd been celebrating their engagement, he'd possibly been hooking up with the archer's wife in the garden.

A knock sounded at the door.

Izzy rolled her shoulders. "My masseuse. Even a massage won't relieve all the tension in my body. And then I have to meet with the detective in a room off the lobby. Will need another bloody massage after that." She walked us to the door. "Thanks again for your concern and stopping by to see me."

Biddy and I slipped past the young woman at the door, wearing the spa's aqua-colored uniform. We headed toward the stairway.

"You know darn well Rhona is paying for Izzy's massage when she wouldn't even get one herself." Biddy fumed. "We need to tell her about that credit card before the woman bankrupts her."

"I'm not telling her, if she truly hadn't known about Izzy. The poor woman has enough to deal with right now. She can deny the charges." I eased out a frustrated groan. "One person we wouldn't mind being guilty appears to be the most innocent. I seriously think Izzy loved the jerk. We need to lock ourselves in our room and watch reruns of *Mrs. Brown's Boys* so people stop confiding in us."

I'd never worked so hard to *not* solve a mystery.

Eight

ON THE WAY UP to our room, at the fifth floor we encountered Archie appearing from behind a large tapestry wall hanging. The three elderly women trailed behind him.

"Oh my, that was exciting, Archie." Ava's aunt Fenella's eyes widened behind her red glasses.

"Never been in a secret passageway," the woman with the pink walking cane said.

"To think, Lord Kerr would slip out of the Queen Victoria Suite and liaison with his love Euphemia via the tunnel." The lady in a brown curly wig wore a wistful look.

And a thief and a killer might have used the passageway to flee the scene of the crime.

The lady with the cane smiled at us. "Hope you lassies are enjoying yerselves."

I nodded. "It's a wonderful hotel."

"Aye, isn't it now?" Fenella said. "A shame about the murder." She shook her head. "After all the hard work Rhona and Ava put into planning the gathering. Such a shame."

A bigger loss than Malcolm apparently.

"Rhona is a lovely woman and still a part of this family," the brown-wig lady said.

"Aye, she is and always will be. We should buy her a wee gift while we're in town shopping."

"What a lovely idea," Fenella said. "Chocolates or a nice selection of teas. We best be going. Our taxi will be here shortly."

The ladies didn't appear concerned about not being available for Detective Henderson's questioning. Archie and the women wished us a lovely day and were off to shop.

Biddy and I peeked behind the tapestry at the faint outline of a door without a handle.

"Too bad we can't open the door, or we could check out the secret passageway," Biddy said. "Thought Ian said it came out on the second floor?"

"He mentioned there's more than one passage. Unless he hadn't wanted us to know this one came out by the Queen Victoria Suite. Yet even if the thief used the passageway to escape with the arrow, the person could have been staying on any guest floor."

"Stopping by for a spot of tea?" Rhona said, appearing down the short hallway and startling us. "That's so sweet of you."

So much for a *Mrs. Brown's Boys* marathon and remaining ignorant.

"I could certainly use the company." She eased out a shaky breath. "Finally got ahold of Sienna. What a dreadful conversation." Her trembling hand couldn't get the key into the lock, so I helped her open the door.

The suite's sitting area was twice the size of our room. A gilded-framed portrait of Queen Victoria and Prince Albert hung on the yellow wall over an ornately carved wooden fireplace. Open red drapes showcased two yellow-padded window seats looking out over the woods.

"Ava told me to ring her after I broke the news to Sienna, but I don't wish to bother her. She was up with me much of the night. Have a seat." She gestured to the red upholstered chairs and couch with cream-colored throw pillows. "I'll be right out." She went into the bedroom and closed the door.

Rather than sitting, we snooped around. An open doorway in the corner led into a tiny circular room with stone walls. Red drapes hung on a small window, and an antique wooden desk and chair filled the space.

Biddy stepped into the nook. "This is the interior of a tower. How cool is that?"

"Totally." Next to a laptop and printer on the desk, a real estate flyer with a familiar home caught my eye. "Hours after her husband's death, and his family home is already on the market?"

Biddy shrugged. "When my uncle Martin died, my auntie Ruth made a donation to the ladies' church group to plan the funeral, not even a wake. The meal had sandwiches and crisps. That was it. No cake or biscuits. Auntie Ruth didn't show—she hopped the first flight to Portugal."

We wandered back out into the sitting room. A wooden credenza displayed coffee and tea service, including four Queen Victoria purple china teacups.

"Ah, grand," Biddy said. "We can drink tea rather than wine from the cups."

We sat down on the couch as the bedroom door swung open. Rhona had exchanged her jeans and sweater for blue leggings, an oversized cream-colored sweatshirt, and blue wool socks. She filled the water kettle and flipped the switch.

"Quite a lovely room, isn't it?" Rhona said. "Certainly a bit pricey. Malcolm was all about the best regardless of the cost and not having anything to show for it." Her gaze darkened. "Yet in the end, it's an investment in the castle. Precisely what I want, but Malcolm hadn't. Rather ironic."

"You plan to invest?" I asked innocently, unsure if Archie should have confided in us about her financial matters.

She smiled. "Yes, I do."

I fought the urge to tell her about Malcolm and his mistress's credit card in case she seriously hadn't a clue. Not wanting to be the bearer of bad news, I'd tell Ava and let her break it to Rhona.

"We'd agreed once Sienna was off to university I could go to work. I needed a sense of purpose. Malcolm claimed the hotel wasn't a good investment. Actually, he didn't think *I* was a good investment. I told him to try to stop me."

Had he tried and that was why *she'd* stopped *him*, permanently?

The tea kettle whistled. Rhona prepared Scottish breakfast tea in the Queen Victoria cups. Biddy and I raved about how much we loved the teacups. Rhona set the tea service and ginger biscuits on the cocktail table. She sat on the love seat and curled her feet under her legs.

"I was tired of Malcolm never taking my advice and treating me like a dimwit. So I asked Ian and Tavish to invest."

Was Tavish there to research his future investment rather than because of Malcolm's death? And was Rhona selling her house to invest? Interesting that Archie had claimed Malcolm had decided to invest prior to his death.

"Malcolm was angry, to say the least."

Rather than tossing the TV out the fifth-story window, had he gone and proposed to Izzy?

"I always expected Malcolm would die of a heart attack or a stroke due to the man's anger and inability to handle stress."

She'd likely held out hope that he'd kick the bucket years ago so she wouldn't have to deal with a messy divorce.

"We were once on a flight to New York, and Malcolm lost it because the plane ran out of his favorite whiskey. He demanded a partial refund on his first-class ticket. He threatened the captain, so the plane diverted to Iceland. He was on two airlines' no-fly lists." Her cheeks reddened. She took a sip of tea and relaxed back against the love seat. "Ava and I left the site inspection filled with ideas on how to help Archie land back on his feet." She smiled. "Besides investing, we're going to help increase the hotel's special-events business. An untapped market Archie hasn't actively pursued."

Malcolm's death appeared to have a healing effect on Rhona. The woman no longer smelled like Grandpa Murray, and she didn't appear to be heavily medicated from too many antianxiety meds. Maybe killing Malcolm had been a survival tactic. The man ultimately would have been the death of her.

A knock sounded at the door.

"That's probably Detective Henderson. He offered to meet up here rather than in the boardroom." She opened the door to find the detective holding a mug with steam rising from it.

He eyed Biddy and me. "Ah, we meet again. Wish everyone was as easy to track down as ye two lassies. Thanks again for your earlier information."

"Sorry we couldn't have been more helpful." My gaze darted from the detective to Rhona. "We had no real clues to provide." I gave her a reassuring smile.

"Should ye think of anything else, ye have my card."

"You mean if we think of *anything*, since we didn't have much to share when we talked and still don't," Biddy said.

We left, the detective wearing a baffled expression.

"We need to get a grip," I said. "We're making ourselves look as guilty as the killer, which I can't imagine is Rhona. I sense she planned to divorce Malcolm once Sienna graduated college. And if Rhona was having an affair with Ian, why would she murder her husband over his affair?"

"To avoid a messy divorce."

"Why take the chance of going to prison for life when she was almost free from him?"

Biddy nodded. "I could have seen Malcolm shooting someone with an arrow, but not Rhona. Especially not with her fibromyalgia."

Unless suffering from a flare-up and unable to shoot an arrow had been an act to make her appear less suspicious.

We hadn't eaten since breakfast and had prepaid the afternoon tea, so we went down to the library lounge. The waiter agreed to box up our goodies to go. We requested double the desserts and no sandwiches, in need of some serious comfort food. We said hello to several family members as we made a beeline for a secluded corner table. Archie entered the room and delivered a teapot to a couple.

I discreetly eyed the owner. "Why'd Archie claim Malcolm had decided to invest when he hadn't? What if he figured with Malcolm dead, Rhona would be free to invest, so he killed him?"

"Haven't a clue, and we're best off not knowing."

Archie glanced over at me, and I gazed off into space. Nothing like being obvious. He headed toward our table.

Biddy's gaze darted around the room. "Where is the bloody waiter with our box of sweets?"

Archie joined us. "I must apologize."

"No worries." Biddy waved off his concern. "Don't think another thing of it. You're grand." Even though the man hadn't yet told us why he was apologizing.

"I said earlier that Malcolm was on board with the investment. That wasn't the case. He'd opted not to invest. I feared that would appear to be a motive for me wanting the man dead. However, Rhona is still quite interested and has lined up several more investors."

"If you lied to the police, you might want to rethink your statement," I said. "If they discover the truth, it'll look like you have something to hide."

Did he?

He nodded, dropping down onto the chair next to us.

Seriously? Where was that waiter?

"I understand if you no longer wish to be involved with the cemetery restoration project."

"I'm still interested. I've actually been thinking of some ideas. Plan to get you a proposal within a few weeks."

"Splendid." His phone rang in his jacket pocket, and he excused himself.

The waiter finally returned with our box of goodies. We were preparing to leave when Tavish approached our table. He looked well rested and freshly showered, yet his five o'clock shadow had gained a few hours.

He pulled up a chair. "I wanted to apologize for earlier."

Biddy wore a strained smile, and I could read her mind.

What do we look like? Bloody priests in a confessional?

"I was a wee bit harsh about Malcolm's death. Was out of sorts after forty hours without sleep. Still can't say I'm broken up over it, but I feel bad for Sienna losing her father in such a brutal way." He slipped an unlit cigarette from behind his ear and twirled it between his fingers. "I hadn't spoken to my brother for almost two years before catching him with my wife. Then I had a few choice words for him."

"Rhona must have been upset about the affair." I was fishing for clues.

He shook his head. "I never told her. Nobody did."

Same as everyone, he claimed Rhona had been ignorant.

"She was merely biding her time until Sienna graduated from uni. Why upset her? It wasn't Malcolm's first affair. It was Izzy's, as far as I know." He frowned. "Living in the remote wilderness wasn't Izzy's thing."

"Didn't she know that when she married you?" Biddy said.

"Aye, we both knew it. But when you're in lust, it doesn't matter. You want to be together no matter what the cost."

His curious gaze narrowed on the window, peering down at the front drive. "Garrett Maxwell?"

I looked out at the man rounding the corner toward the archery course and nodded. "He's the hotel's archer. You know him?"

"Aye, unfortunately, I do." He scowled. "It's been at least twenty years. Garrett, Malcolm, and I were in the same archery club. Garrett is probably the only man I've ever met who was more fiercely competitive than my brother."

Had Malcolm been upset about the hotel selection because his archenemy worked there rather than because it hadn't met his unrealistic standards? Not to mention, Garrett was a bit of a celebrity in the archery world. Maybe the man had flaunted his success in Malcolm's face.

"Malcolm accused Garrett of pinching his lucky, and pricey, bow right before a competition."

"Why would Garrett do that if they were on the same team?"

"In the same *club*, not a team. They were always fighting for the spotlight."

"Do you think Garrett did steal it, or was Malcolm merely trying to get him kicked out of the club?"

"Charges were filed. The bow was never found, so not enough evidence to convict the man." He brushed a finger over his scarred eyebrow. "I'd say he did it."

"I wonder if Detective Henderson is aware of their past?" I said.

"Doubt it. I haven't spoken to him, and I can't imagine anyone else here even realized the two knew each other." He tucked the cigarette behind his ear. "I'll be sure to fill him in on it."

Had Malcolm and Garrett's argument in the garden been about a long-standing feud rather than Charlotte? Yet Malcolm sleeping with his enemy's wife would have been sweet revenge.

Nine

IT WAS TOO gorgeous to sit inside and enjoy our desserts, so we decided to find a secluded bench in the garden. We headed out the front entrance and around the castle. As we neared the back, Detective Henderson's voice carried over from the garden, along with Garrett's. We crouched down and scurried over to the shrub fence.

"We can't say anything to the detective in front of Garrett," I whispered. "I'm not about to tick the guy off and end up later with an arrow in my chest."

"He wouldn't be stupid enough to kill the same way twice, would he?"

"I'm not taking a chance. Besides, maybe the detective already knows Garrett and Malcolm's history together."

"When do you think your wife will be available for questioning?" the detective asked.

"The doctor prescribed antianxiety and sleeping medication. She might be out awhile."

Antianxiety meds for what? Not being allowed to yank

the arrow out of Malcolm's chest? She hadn't seemed a bit traumatized over having found a dead body.

"Please have her ring me when she's awake. I need to speak with her as soon as possible."

"He's leaving," Biddy whispered.

I scuttled like a crab away from the shrubs and over to the cemetery path. Izzy was stretching on a yoga mat under a tree on the lawn, unaware of my presence. It was a good sign that she'd gotten out for some fresh air rather than popping pills with champagne in her room.

I did some yoga breathing and called the detective. He answered, and I quickly filled him in on Garrett and Malcolm's shared history. We hung up.

So much for not getting involved in the investigation. However, something irked me about Garrett Maxwell. He reminded me of Malcolm. And I wanted him to be guilty rather than a Murray family member.

"Mr. Maxwell," the detective called across the garden as Garrett was about to walk out.

The man turned around, and Biddy and I ducked down behind several bushes, peeking over the tops.

"He didn't see us, did he?" Biddy whispered.

I shrugged.

"You failed to mention that ye and the victim were previously acquainted," the detective said.

"Who told you that?" Garrett demanded.

I held my breath while Biddy squeezed the life out of my hand.

"One of my officers just rang. It came up in the background check he's conducting."

Biddy smiled. "Fair play to ya, *Officer* Murray."

"I didn't see how it was relevant," Garrett said. "And still don't. Been over twenty years since I'd seen the bloke."

"Everything is relevant in a murder investigation. Tell me about your relationship with him."

"We were in the same archery club. Didn't much like him, but then, not many did."

"He accused ye of stealing his prized bow."

"*Wrongly* accused me."

"Yet there appeared to have been enough evidence to file a charge against you."

"The charge was dropped." Garrett heaved an impatient sigh. "If there's nothing else, I have a lesson in five minutes."

"That's all for now."

Garrett headed toward the archery course. Biddy and I popped up from behind the bushes, startling the detective. We gave him a thumbs-up, which he returned with a smile, then headed off.

"If Garrett stole the arrow, he knew the value," Biddy said. "Why would he use it to kill Malcolm?"

"Heat of the moment. His temper is right up there with Malcolm's. Anger makes a person irrational. We best warn Tavish to have his back. If Garrett runs into him, he's going to think he snitched to the police."

"Better than him thinking it was us. Tavish would be able to protect himself more than we would."

"From an arrow whizzing through the air at a hundred and fifty miles per hour? I don't trust Garrett not to use the same method in a second murder. Any murder would be suspicious at this point."

Biddy placed a hand to her chest. "Do you think a leather chest protector could be stopping an arrow?"

"I think the only thing that could stop an arrow would be Detective Henderson tossing Garrett Maxwell in the slammer."

I spent the rest of the afternoon taking photos of the cemetery for the restoration project's Facebook page and my website. Biddy made a last-minute appointment for a facial. After Dad and Ian returned to the hotel early evening, we joined them in the library for a drink.

They were the only ones in the lounge, seated at a window table, drinking another local craft beer Ian had recommended. Both were dressed in tan khakis and blue polo shirts with the Saint Andrews Links logo. They looked like best buds. I smiled. It was the happiest I'd seen Dad since Mom's death.

Ian gave Biddy and me each a gorgeous green tweed purse with the course logo embroidered on the front. We slipped the purses on our shoulders, trying them on for size.

"This is lovely," Biddy said. "Wonder if the Duchess of Cambridge had a similar handbag during her uni days there."

"Speaking of which," Dad said. "Had the driver stop at a souvenir shop." He handed us each a large tin with William and Kate's wedding photo on top and filled with fudge. "The fudge is made on the Royal Yacht *Britannia*."

"Now we can eat royal fudge while drinking from our Queen Victoria teacups." I opened the tin and set it on the table to share. The flavors included caramel, triple-decker (a trio of chocolate, caramel, and vanilla), rum raisin, and chocolate-orange swirl. Biddy and I still hadn't polished off the box of desserts from afternoon tea. Yet I popped a piece of chocolate-orange swirl into my mouth.

"How did you lassies get on today?" Ian asked.

Since Tavish would undoubtedly fill Ian in on his Garrett Maxwell sighting and the man's history with Malcolm, I shared the information with them. I asked Ian to let Tavish know we'd spoken to the detective.

"Strange that Malcolm hadn't mentioned knowing Garrett," Ian said. "Both of 'em acted like they'd just met at the archery competition."

"Well, Garrett admitted to Detective Henderson that he'd known Malcolm from the archery club years ago."

Ian's gaze narrowed. "If Malcolm had seen the bloke for the first time in twenty years, I can't imagine he'd have taken it so calmly that nobody would have known."

I nodded. "Why would both men have pretended not to recognize each other?"

Dad eyed me. "That's a question for Detective Henderson to figure out. Not Cagney and Lacey."

"Who?" I asked.

"Never mind. It was before your time. Point is, you and Biddy best be careful and stay away from that Garrett."

"We will. Besides, he doesn't know it was us that told Detective Henderson about his past with Malcolm." Fingers crossed the man hadn't seen us in the garden earlier.

"Ian mentioned he offered to be our personal tour guide in Edinburgh," Dad said.

"Aye, already planning the itinerary. A graveyard, filming location, and a pub that brews its own beer. Could add the Royal Yacht *Britannia*, docked in Edinburgh and open for tours. The souvenir shop has the Queen Victoria china collection."

"Collection?" Biddy said. "Not merely a teacup?"

Ian shook his head. "Bought my auntie a lovely teapot for her birthday."

We clinked our pewter wineglasses against the men's beer bottles, toasting our future stay in Edinburgh.

Dad set down his empty bottle. "I better have only one so I'm sharp for breakfast bingo."

"Hope it's not like my last bingo nightmare." Biddy shook her head. "Bachelorette bingo for my friend's hen party. We were out clubbing and had to do things like use the men's loo, do a pole dance, and call the groom. The drunk maid of honor speed-dialed the groom. Not only was the bride-to-be surprised that her friend knew her fiancé's number, but that he was on speed-dial. Turned out her fiancé had been shagging her maid of honor. Things turned ugly real fast."

Hopefully, no family secrets were exposed during our reunion bingo. Especially not mine.

Two hours later Biddy and I were dressed in our jammies. I sat on my bed bouncing cemetery restoration ideas off her while we polished off the last desserts in the box.

"I'll set up a Facebook page so people can follow the project. With one click of a button, a person can sign up for the Adopt-a-Grave program. Getting locals involved will ensure that the cemetery is looked after on a regular basis.

Each volunteer will receive the history of the person buried in the adopted grave."

Biddy licked raspberry tart crumbs from her fingers. "Everyone will be fighting over Euphemia's grave."

"I know. I'm thinking about having different donation tiers. Premium graves like Euphemia's and Lord Kerr's would cost more than tiers two and three."

"I'd want Princess Beatrice's grave, the one you told me about. In memory of our kitty. Pet graves should be tier two. Animal lovers will be mad for it."

"Maybe a local shelter or humane society would want to organize volunteers for the pet cemetery. Part of the donations could go to the organization and part to the hotel." My fingers flew across the keyboard, documenting our ideas. "The more people involved, the more exposure for the castle."

A knock sounded at the door.

Biddy popped up from her bed. "Our first visitor."

It was nearly midnight.

I removed the empty dessert box from the end of the bed so the person would have somewhere to sit.

Biddy opened the door and greeted Ava.

"What perfect timing." I patted the end of my bed for Ava to have a seat. "We were just brainstorming ideas for the cemetery restoration project. Not sure if Archie mentioned it to you."

Ava nodded. "What a lovely idea." Yet she didn't appear enthused, taking a tentative step into the room. "Sorry to call in so late. I saw the light on under your door. I hope it's okay."

"No worries," Biddy said. "We're up all hours of the night."

Ava sat on the end of my bed. Biddy plopped down on hers.

"Is everything okay?" I asked.

"It's about my DNA test results." She stared down at her fingers fidgeting with the silk Murray tartan scarf tied around her neck. "The one time I should have listened to Malcolm. He told me not to take the test."

I gave her a sympathetic look, grabbing my fudge tin from the nightstand and placing it on the bed next to her. "I know, people aren't always prepared for what their results may reveal."

"I certainly wasn't." She popped a piece of fudge into her mouth. "I haven't told Rhona, but I feel I need to tell the police even though it might make her look guiltier. If the police somehow discover this, I'll be in trouble for not having disclosed the information. Or if a distant DNA match figures it out, they might tell the police."

"You have to tell the detective if you think it might impact the case," I said.

She nodded, meeting my gaze for the first time since entering the room. "You haven't signed into your Ancestry.com account since I received my test results."

I'd been too busy finalizing a client's research and preparing for this trip to worry about my own research. Now, I was worried. Where was she going with this? The hairs on the back of my neck prickled.

"When our grandmother Murray died nearly twenty-eight years ago, Malcolm didn't make it back from Chicago for the funeral. I was so upset that it has stuck in my head all these years."

Twenty-eight years ago Malcolm was in Chicago?

My heart raced. "What are you saying?"

"Since our shared Murray matches are distant relations, I figured you didn't know." Her pained expression reminded me of the time Dad had to break the news that my gerbil, Max, had died when I was at camp. "I think Malcolm was...your father."

Biddy gasped in horror. "Janey."

I sat paralyzed while the room started spinning.

"I should have approached you the night of the reception. I feel horrible bringing it up now."

She should feel horrible bringing it up *ever*!

I shook my head vigorously. "No way. Absolutely no way was Malcolm my father." I stuffed a piece of caramel fudge into my mouth and then another.

Ava wore an apologetic look. "We share the correct amount of DNA for that match."

I continued shaking my head. "There are numerous relationship possibilities based on that amount of shared DNA. Maybe it's not even my account you were looking at."

"Margaret Catherine Murray, Ireland Midlands."

"Janey," Biddy muttered, snagging several pieces of fudge from the tin.

"Could easily be more than one person with my profile name and location." I grabbed my laptop and signed into my DNA account. Near the top of my matches under *Close Family*, Ava's smiling profile pic stared back at me. My heart went berserk. "We only share seven hundred and fifty cM. Not enough for you to be my aunt." My shoulders relaxed slightly. Yet it was still about seven hundred cM more than Dad likely shared with his second cousin, whom I supposedly wasn't even related to!

"My brothers and I don't share the same mother," Ava said.

"This could still mean a lot of things."

Like the testing company had royally messed up!

I pulled up Ancestry.com's list of Ava's and my possible relationships. "Rather than a half aunt, you could be a great-grandparent or grandaunt. And there's a two percent chance you're a half first cousin. Lots of possibilities."

Yet none were as plausible as a half aunt!

I scrolled down farther to see if Dad had reactivated his account and now showed up as a distant relation. When I'd received my results and he hadn't been at the top of my matches, I hadn't looked further. What if he'd appeared as a distant relative? Now, he wasn't showing up, apparently not having reactivated his account.

Ava placed a comforting hand on my arm. "I'm so sorry. This must be an awful shock."

"If you tell the police, this could definitely make Rhona look guiltier." It could also make Dad look guilty if Malcolm was indeed my... My stomach tossed. It might seem suspicious that Malcolm had been killed after seeing us for the first time in twenty years. That Dad had discovered Malcolm's relationship to me and snapped. What if Dad went from being at the bottom of the suspect list to the top?

"Have you mentioned this to anyone?" I asked.

She shook her head.

"Please don't. Give me time to figure out how to tell my dad, and maybe the detective will have identified the killer."

Ava agreed to give me the following day. She left, and I collapsed against the bed.

"Janey," Biddy muttered.

"Please say something besides *Janey*."

Unable to come up with any words of comfort, Biddy handed me her tin of fudge.

"I need something stronger than that." Yet I stuffed two pieces into my mouth.

She grabbed the souvenir Clan Murray bottle of Scotch, opened it, and handed it to me. I took a swig and gagged.

"I feel like puking even without drinking that stuff. I better stick with fudge."

Biddy paced the short distance between our beds and the desk. "Let's not panic."

"The panic ship has already sailed and sunk. I'm now boarding the *SS Meltdown*."

"Like you said, that amount of shared DNA could mean a lot of possible connections to Ava, right?"

I pressed a hand against my forehead to keep it from exploding across the room. "I can't think." I returned to Ancestry.com and pulled up Ava's family tree. "Her grandma Murray died just over eight months before I was born. There's an obituary attached confirming the date. I'd have to have been born early."

"And maybe your mom lied about her due date just in case someone learned about the affair."

The affair that never happened, because there was another reason for this shared DNA! I'd promised Dad I'd work harder at forgiving Mom, but that was now out the window. How could my mother have cheated on Dad with such a despicable man? Right under my family's own roof! I slammed my laptop shut.

"Holy cats," I muttered.

"What?"

"Rhona and I were talking about my birthday yesterday afternoon before Malcolm was killed. What if she figured out that I'd been born nearly nine months after Malcolm's visit to Chicago and his grandma's funeral?"

"What's the chance she'd recall the date her husband's grandmother died? I couldn't even tell you the year of my own grandparents' deaths. Besides, I doubt Malcolm and Rhona were married at that time, so it wouldn't have been like he was cheating on her. Unless Sienna is our age and started university late."

I shoved aside thoughts of that horrible man with my mom! My breathing was so rapid I was on the verge of hyper-ventilating. I ran over and threw open a window. When the fresh air didn't calm my breathing, I crawled onto the tower, where a brisk wind slapped me in the face.

"Stop!" Biddy scurried out the window and onto the tower, grabbing my arm. "Don't do it. I can't live without you."

I shrugged free from her grasp. "I'm not jumping. I'm trying to breathe."

Biddy threw her arms around me and gave me a big hug.

"Still...can't...breathe."

She released her hold. "Sorry."

I eased several calming breaths in and out until my heart rate slowed. "I'm not sharing any of this with my dad until I figure it out. He must not have recalled Malcolm's visit, or he'd have had some inkling. He wouldn't have lied about not knowing who my father might be."

"Even if it was Malcolm?"

I nodded. "He'd never have invited me here without telling me his suspicions."

"Maybe he didn't have suspicions until Malcolm reminded him about having visited that time."

"We have to find the killer before my dad becomes a prime suspect."

"Or you do. Horrified over having discovered Malcolm was your father, you could have killed him in the heat of the moment. We keep saying this wasn't a planned murder."

"Gee, just when I thought I couldn't feel any worse. Thankfully, I have an alibi. My dad doesn't. And if this is true, which I pray it isn't, that moves my dad to the top of the suspect list. We need to make sure Garrett Maxwell remains the number-one suspect. Not only on our list, but the detective's."

If it turned out the archer wasn't guilty, I'd have to be responsible for a Murray family member, *my* family member, going to prison. Better one of them than my dad.

Ten

THE FOLLOWING MORNING, I was showered and dressed by 6:00 a.m., not having slept a wink. Biddy was still in bed with the quilt pulled over her head.

"Get showered." I threw back the quilt.

She rolled over and buried her face in the pillow.

"We have a killer to catch before my dad becomes a prime suspect." I dropped down onto my bed. "It looks bad that everyone else wanted Malcolm dead most of their lives and then he happens to get murdered two days after seeing my dad and me for the first time in years. The detective brought up the fact, so he's already suspicious!"

Biddy rolled away from the pillow, squinting back the light from the desk lamp. "Fine. I get it. You're anxious to catch a killer. So am I. But breakfast doesn't even open for an hour. We're still on holiday and shouldn't be getting up before the sun does."

"It gives us time to put together a game plan to prove Garrett or someone is guilty."

Seized with inspiration, Biddy popped up in bed. "Breakfast bingo. What a perfect way to discover clues."

"Unless there's a square that asks you to find someone who has shot a man with an arrow, I doubt bingo will help us gather evidence."

Biddy rolled her eyes. "We can make up our own squares. Like...find someone who can disassemble a recurve bow in under a minute."

"Yeah, that's much more discreet." I dropped back against the headboard. "There's no way my dad knew about Malcolm being my..." I swallowed the icky taste in my mouth, unable to utter the word. "Unless he figured it out since we got here. Even if Malcolm mentioned his visit twenty-eight years ago and my dad put two and two together, no way would he have killed him over it."

Would the police be as confident about his innocence?

"I never should have taken that stupid DNA test. How am I going to tell my dad that my mom had an affair with...that man? Dad's getting on so great with the family, especially Ian. He's the happiest I've seen him in a long time. I can't ruin that."

Biddy shrugged. "His relationship with them might be ruined anyway if one of them goes to prison for murder. Malcolm being your...relation would also strengthen the motive for Rhona, Ava, and Ian."

"If Rhona had figured it out when we were talking about my birthday, she'd likely have confided in Ian, furious that her husband had cheated on her from early in the marriage. If indeed they were married at the time. But why kill him now when he'd likely cheated their entire marriage?"

"Because no other affair had produced an illegitimate child."

"A *known* illegitimate child."

"If Malcolm and Rhona weren't married at the time, maybe she was afraid you'd try to get money out of him. So she killed him off before either of you figured it out. I doubt she'd have a reason to kill you next..."

I sprang from the bed. "Stop trying to cheer me up and hop in the shower."

"Well, we need to be watching our backs if Rhona thought your purpose for attending the reunion was to meet your biological father. And if her motive is increased, so is Ian's. I get the feeling he'd do anything to protect her."

"What would Ava's motive be?"

"She's wanted to kill him since her tenth birthday party. I'm sure she has plenty of motives. And when she realized you were her brother's, er, relation, that provided her with the perfect opportunity to off him and point the finger at your dad."

"I can't believe she'd do such a thing."

"You can't trust someone you've only known two days. You can't trust anyone right now."

I nodded. "We also can't say anything to make my dad suspicious. We need to make sure he can establish a concrete alibi. And try to verify if Ava is correct about the time period of Malcolm's visit to Chicago. Maybe she'd been so distraught over her grandmother's death she's not remembering it correctly."

I, for one, wanted to forget ever having known about his visit.

The breakfast room wasn't as lively ten minutes after it opened as it was ten minutes before it *closed*, when Biddy and I usually arrived. Archie wasn't yet at the door greeting guests. Even the three elderly aunts weren't there enjoying their morning tea. Dressed in his running clothes, Dad occupied the only table, next to a window overlooking the garden and the path leading to the archery course.

My phone call had taken him by surprise when he was returning from his run.

I plopped two tea bags into a china cup and grabbed two butteries. After this trip, I'd have to have my cholesterol tested for the first time.

We joined Dad at the table, where he was drinking a glass of tomato juice.

"Surprised you girls are up so early, or did you just not go to bed?" Dad chuckled.

Biddy and I let out nervous giggles. I shot her a discreet glance. We needed to get a grip!

"It sounded like your golf outing went great yesterday." I slathered jam on the bottom of a buttery.

Dad nodded. "Was great spending time with Ian after all these years. And was good for him to get away from the castle. Even though he and Malcolm weren't close, it's still a shock to have your brother murdered and for you to be a suspect."

I choked down a bite of the flaky pastry. "Why would *I* be a suspect?"

Dad's gaze narrowed. "I meant *Ian* when I said *you*. Think you best take a nap before we head into the village this morning. This whole thing is taking its toll on all of us." He took a drink of juice. "Sure makes you think about how quickly it all can end. You might consider working on your relationship with your sisters. Life is too short to not be getting along."

I nodded faintly. As if forgiving Mom and keeping Dad out of prison wasn't enough to deal with right now.

"I'm going to give Adam a call," Dad said. "Haven't talked to him in almost a year."

Dad and his brother were never close, but they got along. They coexisted.

"How did your chat go with Detective Henderson yesterday?" Biddy asked.

He shrugged. "Fine. Didn't have much to tell him."

"Outside of your alibi?" I said.

"Not much of an alibi since I was alone in my room."

I nonchalantly spread jam on my buttery. "You must have been on the phone or a video conference with work, or emailing, or something." A sense of desperation filled my voice.

"I promised you no work that day, and I stuck to it." Dad smiled proudly.

Why had he chosen that day to listen to me about cutting back on work?

"If you didn't call work, maybe you checked in with Mia or Emma at that time or called room service."

Dad's gaze narrowed. "I'm not too worried about having a stronger alibi. I hadn't seen the man for nearly twenty years. Why would I have wanted to kill him?"

My heart raced. "Prisons are filled with thousands of innocent people."

Dad placed a calming hand on mine. "Mags, relax. I'm not going to prison." He rested back in his chair. "Speaking of alibis, thankfully Rhona and Ava can alibi each other. Rhona certainly had the most reasons for wanting the man dead."

The women's alibi was suspicious, to say the least. If needed, I would have to disprove their alibi to move them to the top of the suspect list rather than Dad. Maybe they were in on the murder together.

"Hope it wasn't the poor woman." Dad stood. "I'm going to go shower so I'm ready to head into Dalwade after bingo."

I needed to stay here and find a killer, though spending time with Dad might help me figure out how to strengthen his alibi. And it would look suspicious if I didn't go into town.

Dad walked off, and Biddy smacked my arm. "Worried about *me* slipping up and saying something I shouldn't, are ya?"

I sucked in a calming breath. "I know. I need to get a grip."

On his way out, Dad crossed paths with Ian, and the men chatted a few minutes. I nibbled nervously on a buttery, hoping they would still be as friendly once Dad discovered Ian was my uncle. Ian grabbed an espresso and joined us, in better spirits than he had been yesterday at breakfast.

"Did you happen to mention my conversation with Detective Henderson to Tavish?" I asked him.

"Nay. He wasn't in my room last night. Probably went for a dram at the local pub. He was snoring away on the couch this morning. Figured he needed sleep. Will tell him about it when he gets up."

"How long have you lived in Edinburgh?" Biddy asked.

"Nearly twenty years."

She nodded. "Where exactly is the Murray home you grew up in?"

The stately home that hadn't been part of my past and wouldn't be part of my future either. Even if Rhona wasn't selling the place, I had no desire to visit it.

Was Ian aware that Rhona was selling the home?

"A rural area north of Stirling. Malcolm bought us out of our shares after our parents passed away." He arched a curious brow. "Are these questions preparing you for bingo?"

Biddy shrugged. "Just trying to even the playing ground. I'm at a bit of a disadvantage, just having met everyone."

His parents' deaths were the perfect segue to his grandma's funeral.

"I inherited my grandma's home in Ireland when she passed away last Christmas. Of course, my sisters felt they should have received a share of it even though they rarely ever visited Ireland or stayed in touch with her."

Ian nodded in understanding.

"They didn't even come over to Ireland for her funeral."

"Malcolm didn't make it back from the States for our grandma Murray's funeral."

"Oh, how long ago did she pass away?" I asked.

He peered into his espresso cup. "I'm bloody awful with dates. Must have been at least twenty-five years ago."

Try nearly twenty-eight years ago. According to her obituary, she died in January 1994, not quite nine months before I was born. And sadly, Ava was right that Malcolm was in the

States—but maybe he wasn't in *Chicago*. Grandma had always said coincidences happened more often than you'd think in genealogy research. That had better be true with my family line.

"Ava was raging that Malcolm received the same inheritance as the rest of us when he didn't even care enough to attend the funeral."

"My sisters would have sold my grandma's cottage to the highest bidder without giving it a second thought."

"No matter how much money Malcolm had, he'd have always wanted more. Do feel a bit bad that one of my last conversations with him was an argument."

At the archery team-building event when Malcolm had gone off on Rhona, or another argument after that?

Ian glanced at his watch. "It's almost bingo time. Then I have an investors' meeting with Archie and the others. This place has a lot of potential. Just needs some attention."

"Rhona mentioned investing," I said. "Why do you think Malcolm didn't want to invest?"

Ian frowned. "Because he'd need to be hands on and put effort into renovating the hotel and growing the business. Malcolm would have rather sat at his cushy desk playing the stock market. He always looked for an easy way out."

Death certainly wasn't an easy way out.

Dad returned when Ava was distributing bingo cards. The game required you to find a family member who matched the description in each square.

"Find someone who has been on TV." Biddy glanced around our table. "If you have that square, I'd be happy to autograph it for you." She told Ian about our previous and upcoming episode on *Rags to Riches Roadshow*.

Ian looked impressed. "Didn't realize I'm among celebrities. Please sign my card 'To Ian, the wittiest man I know.'" He grinned, handing her his bingo card.

"Of course, dahling," Biddy said, scrawling her autograph on the card. "I could also sign *find someone who has been to more than one foreign country.*"

"A person is only allowed to sign one square per card," I said. "The purpose is to mingle."

"Well, you can sign for someone who was named after an ancestor." Biddy glanced at Ian. "Mags was named after her granny Margaret Fitzsimmons."

I signed everyone's cards, then began circulating around the room. The most intriguing square was to find someone with a family heirloom dating back more than two centuries. Aunt Fenella seemed like a good bet, so I headed to her.

The woman's porcelain cheeks went as red as her glasses. "It should have been a Georgian mahogany clock dated eighteen hundred. However, upon my dear brother's death, he gave it to his son Malcolm despite our mother requesting that it go to me when he died. Malcolm sold it."

"That's horrible." Just when I'd thought it was impossible to despise the man more. I couldn't imagine selling off Grandma's gold locket, my only family heirloom.

"He didn't even offer us an opportunity to purchase the items, claiming we'd have wanted a deal rather than paying fair market value." Fenella's red lips pressed into a thin line.

Even dead Malcolm still made my blood boil. Blood that likely shared that horrible man's DNA!

"To not even give you the chance to buy them." I shook my head in disgust. "What an awful thing to do."

"The man didn't have a sentimental bone in his body.

Was nasty since the day he was born. I minded him as a wee bairn. Always throwing temper tantrums." Her look said tsk, tsk. "Some things never changed. Except now that he's dead." Her gray eyes twinkled. "I do have a lovely Chamberlain Worcester coffee cup made for the Marquess of Queensbury, dated circa 1815."

I handed her my card to sign. I signed her square for someone who'd lived in more than one country. Fenella moved on. I peered around the room. Ava and I exchanged awkward glances. Being the only two available players, she headed my way. Heart racing, I plastered on a pleasant smile, as did she.

Ava scanned her card. "Never had a speeding ticket?"

"One. But in my defense, I was following my dad and merely trying to keep up with him. He paid my ticket."

"Ever ridden on a motorcycle?"

I shook my head.

"Swam in more than one ocean?"

"Only the Atlantic." Actually, I'd fallen off a Jet Ski in the Atlantic when my sister Mia, the driver, took a sharp turn. My arms flailing in the water was more a desperate attempt to get back on the ski before drowning than me swimming.

Ava tapped her pen against the card, avoiding the "free" square in the middle. *Ask someone to share a secret.* She was privy to my biggest secret. However, it was only a matter of time before she learned about my appearance on *Rags to Riches Roadshow* and discovered my other one.

"How about the free square?" I said.

She was taken aback by my suggestion, and her cheeks flushed pink.

"I'm a genealogist."

A relieved look relaxed Ava's features. As if she'd expected me to confess a bigger secret than Malcolm being my father.

"I haven't told anyone here because I was afraid of being asked if I'd researched the Murray family history or had done a DNA test. I mentioned my grandma was a genealogist. That's why I decided on the career."

Ava smiled. "Thanks for telling me. I appreciate it. Maybe you could help me out with our, er, the Murray tree."

I smiled faintly and signed her card.

I quickly scanned my card, wanting to move on to the next person. "Can you make a family recipe by heart?"

"Aye, my grandmother Murray's butteries. Both her family's as well as my grandfather's family recipes." She signed my card. "I'd be happy to share them."

"That'd be great."

If I didn't get up the nerve to ask Mia for Grandma's butteries recipe, I could get it from Ava. I assumed our family recipe had come from Grandpa Murray's side since Grandma Murray had been German.

I excused myself and continued circulating, breathing a relieved sigh. Ava was the last person I felt like discussing family with right now.

Despite getting off to a shaky start, the game turned out to be fun and informational. I learned from Ian that Tavish had once ridden a motorcycle across Europe. Ian had studied at the Sorbonne and spoke fluent French. And the elderly aunt with the brown wig had once been in an Andrews Sisters tribute band.

I joined Biddy at the beverage station and made a cup of

tea. I told her about my conversation with Fenella. "I guess we should add her to the list of suspects."

"We can also be adding her sister to the list. Malcolm ran over her cat Esme. She's convinced it wasn't an accident. I'm sure it wasn't." Biddy's grip tightened around the delicate china teacup. "He was more worried about his Mercedes than the poor woman's cat. I thought if anyone was inno-cent, it would be the three aunts."

Rather than identifying Malcolm's killer, we'd added two suspects to our long list.

Eleven

DALWADE WAS a quaint village with a population of a few thousand people. Tea rooms, cafés, and shops lined the main street, including Walker's Woolen Goods. Biddy wrapped a green-and-blue plaid wool scarf around my dad's neck, in addition to the three he was already wearing. She tilted her head to the side, trying to determine if the scarf matched the blue sweater she'd had him try on. Too bad for Dad he was about the same size as Biddy's boyfriend Collin.

Dad's face and neck were bright red, and sweat was beading on his upper lip. "Biddy, I'm dying here." He unwrapped the latest scarf from his neck and tossed it onto the table of sweaters. "The second one goes the best."

"I agree," I said.

Biddy nodded. "I'm still not sure about the sweater size." She wrapped her arms around Dad's neck and peered at the top of his chest.

He gazed off into space. "This is awkward."

"When I have my arms around him, my eyes are level

with his lower neck." She slipped her arms around his waist. "Collin is a bit trimmer."

"I'll have you know I run three miles every morning."

"Go with the large." I pulled Biddy away from Dad. "It's perfect, and if he washes it in the machine, he'll shrink it."

Dad unwrapped the two scarves from his neck and peeled off the sweater. He handed the sweater and recommended scarf to Biddy.

She smiled. "Thanks a mil for being my model."

Dad had always been a good sport. When I was young, he'd wear one of my fancy hats when he attended my tea parties. Mom had once backed out last minute on taking me trick-or-treating, so he'd worn her costume. Well, at least the black wig, since he couldn't fit into the long formfitting dress. After watching the *Addams Family* movie, I'd had my heart set on being Wednesday. Dad had wanted to throw together a Gomez costume, but I'd whined that a suit was lame. That nobody would realize it was even a costume. So he'd worn a previous costume of Mom's, a looser fitting black witch's dress. We won first place in our subdivision's costume contest.

"Now on to your sisters," he said to me.

I trudged over to the women's section with him while Biddy went to check out.

Emma and Mia couldn't care less about visiting Scotland or the Murrays but were all about the gifts. They'd given Dad a list of suggestions. Besides a wool sweater, Mia wanted a cookbook by the Scottish-born celebrity chef Gordon Ramsay. She planned to create his dishes in her ten-thousand-dollar double convection oven. Emma wanted an

Outlander T-shirt and a bottle of Scotch for her husband, Dread Ted.

"Mia wants a green one." He held up a pretty emerald-green sweater with a turtleneck.

"She won't wear anything that touches her neck. And no buttons or zippers."

Drawing my sister's name one year for our family's secret Santa gift exchange had been a complete nightmare. Mia hadn't liked one thing about the gorgeous sweater I'd spent an entire afternoon shopping for, and she'd exchanged it for flannel pajamas.

Dad held up a cream sweater.

"Cream turns her skin yellow. She'll only wear white."

He folded the sweater. "How about I buy her a hat and matching gloves instead?"

"A hat would mess up her hair." I grabbed a green fisherman's sweater with a round collar for Mia and a maroon one for Emma. "These should work."

He smiled. "You were always an easier child to please than your sisters."

I bought Edmond a lovely green wool cap for looking after my house and Pinky. Nothing in the shop really screamed Rosie. The elderly woman's daily attire consisted of a crisply pressed dress and pearls rather than bulky wool clothing. We left Dad to shop for himself and headed down the street to a pharmacy that carried a few souvenirs and postcards. When working my seasonal jobs around the US, I'd always sent Grandma Fitzsimmons a postcard. I was determined to carry on the tradition with others. A card with two sheep, the smaller one asking the other if he was his grandpa, was perfect for Edmond. The man was a history buff and dabbled in genealogy. One with colorful vintage teacups was ideal for Rosie, who worked in her brother's antique shop.

I showed Biddy a card with a scene of sheep trotting up a country road toward a sunset. "How about this for Gretta?"

"Not sure that's appropriate, seeing as she's collecting road rubbish for her community service."

"Suppose not." I chose one with pictures of Scotland's most popular flowers.

We grabbed a to-go cup of tea from a shop and continued down the sidewalk, where we encountered Chloe's. Biddy and I stood there finishing our tea before heading into Izzy's favorite boutique. A boy flew out the door and about plowed us over. Alec, the delivery guy at the castle yesterday.

"So sorry about that," he said, taking a step back. Recognition flickered in his blue eyes, and his brow furrowed. "Also sorry about yesterday. Was nice of ye to help me out with Lily, and then I left without thanking ye."

I smiled. "No worries." I eyed the package in his arm. "Another delivery for the hotel?"

"Nay, for my maw's birthday. Would like to return to the castle though. My mates would be jealous if I get the inside scoop on the first murder in the area in over fifty years." He stared expectantly at us.

Biddy shrugged. "No clue."

He frowned. "Too bad. Hate to think it might turn out to be the bloke's wife."

"Why do you think that?" I asked.

"I was collecting deliveries here two days before he died.

He and that younger red-haired woman ran into his wife right here outside the shop. She was raging."

Biddy shook her head in disgust. "What a horrible way to discover your husband's having an affair, catching them in the act."

Although their act in the cemetery would have been worse.

"Oh, she'd known about the two of 'em but was upset it hadn't ended, like he'd said. Wouldn't have wanted to be that bloke when he got back to the hotel that night. Would have hated to be him even more the next night, with an arrow through his chest."

Biddy and I nodded.

"His wife told the woman she'd better not plan on sticking around. With all the deliveries I've been making, it seems she did. Well, best get to my maw's so I'm back in time for takeaway deliveries." He crossed the street and hopped into a small gray car.

"Isn't that interesting," Biddy said. "Just as we suspected. Rhona had indeed known about the affair for some time, despite everyone repeatedly assuring us she hadn't a clue."

"The more everyone insists she isn't the killer, the more I think she's guilty."

Alec sped off, and a blue BMW pulled into his parking spot. Garrett Maxwell stepped from the car. He peered across the street, and our gazes locked. His look shot daggers, or rather arrows, at me. A gasp caught in my throat.

He knew I was the police informant.

Biddy took a sip of tea. "What's even more interesting is that Rhona isn't a blood relation, yet everyone has come to her rescue."

Garrett was still glaring at me. Heart racing, I grabbed Biddy's arm and whisked her inside Chloe's boutique.

"Janey. What are ya doing?" Biddy wiped tea from the front of her green fleece jacket.

"Sorry. Garrett's out there." Our gazes darted out the store window to the archer peering back at us from across the street. We ducked behind a dress display. "He knows we're the ones who snitched on him to Detective Henderson. I knew he'd seen us." I peeked around the dresses at Garrett heading toward the shop. "Holy cats. He's coming this way."

"At least he doesn't have a bow and arrow."

He didn't need one. He was about to give me a heart attack.

Biddy eyed the tag on a green flirty dress. "This dress is only fifty pounds."

"Can I help you ladies?" a woman said.

Biddy and I let out startled gasps and spun around to face an older woman with beautiful silver hair wearing a blue pantsuit. I glanced over my shoulder at Garrett staring in the window as he continued down the sidewalk. I about fainted with relief.

"A friend of ours recommended your shop," Biddy said.

"How lovely. Who would that be?"

"Ah...a guest at the Dalwade Hotel and Spa."

"Must be Izzy Murray. She's been our best client this week. Actually, this month."

"I can see why." Biddy eyed a display of fashion scarves neatly folded on a table. "You have a lovely shop."

I spied Dad walking out of the woolen goods shop across the street, carrying two large bags.

"We'll be back soon to browse." I grabbed Biddy's arm

and made a beeline for the door. We'd be sticking by Dad's side until we left the village.

Maybe until we boarded our Aer Lingus flight back to Dublin.

Upon returning from Dalwade, Dad suggested tea in the library. The lounge offered complimentary tea and coffee between breakfast and afternoon tea. Following our scary run-in with Garrett Maxwell, I could have used something stronger. However, I needed a clear head to catch a killer. Only ten more hours until midnight, my deadline. Yet Ava likely wouldn't be calling Detective Henderson at the stroke of midnight. I could stay up all night, if needed, to nail the guilty person.

Dad waved to Ava and Rhona, the only other people in the lounge. "Let's join the ladies. I can get everyone's opinions on the gifts I bought."

What fun. An awkward conversation with my *aunt* Ava, who shared the secret of my biological father, while looking at gifts for my two undeserving sisters.

"We're going to pass on tea," I said. "Have to talk to Tavish about my conversation with Detective Henderson yesterday."

I'd told Dad about Malcolm and Garrett's past but hadn't told him about our encounter with Garrett in town. He'd insist we back off and stop investigating, and I couldn't disclose why that wasn't an option. Tavish needed to be aware of Garrett stalking us in case Biddy and I went missing.

Speaking of which, I hadn't seen Tavish since afternoon tea yesterday.

He hadn't had a run-in with Garrett, had he?

And was lying somewhere with an arrow in his chest?

Izzy stormed into the library, wrapped in a spa robe, and stalked across the room to Rhona and Ava's table. "They canceled my massage because my credit card was declined."

Rhona gave Izzy the evil eye. "You mean my late *husband's* credit card? Yes, I reported the spa charges as well as the ones at Chloe's boutique as fraudulent, seeing as they occurred after my husband's death."

"Why am *I* the bad person?" Izzy tossed her arms up in frustration. "I loved Malcolm. You didn't. Why couldn't you just let him go?"

Ava whipped her napkin on the table. "He was her husband, not yours. Stop making a scene. Get dressed, pack your bags, and get the hell out of here. You weren't invited anyway."

"First, Chloe's boutique will be giving you a ring." Rhona's gaze narrowed. "Actually, they won't be giving you a *ring* or any other piece of jewelry. Rather, they'll be wanting your purchases returned, or they'll be filing charges."

Whoa, go Rhona.

Izzy peered over at Biddy and me with a hurt expression. "You had no business telling her about the card. I told you that in confidence. I thought you were my friends."

Friends?

"We didn't tell her about the card." My gaze darted to Rhona. "Sorry. We should have told you about it, but we didn't want to upset you even more. Figured she'd already maxed it out and you could dispute the charges."

"These young ladies didn't tell me about the card," Rhona said. "It was flagged for an excessive number of charges, and the company left a message on Malcolm's voice mail, which I now access."

"You're merely jealous because Malcolm gave me an engagement ring." Izzy held out her hand, showing off her diamond and emerald ring.

Ava surged from her chair. "Give me that ring. It's Rhona's, not yours. She's not paying for it."

"He paid cash," Izzy spat.

Rhona let out a bitter laugh. "Malcolm didn't have cash. We were almost broke."

A glint of surprise flashed in Izzy's green eyes. "No cash that you were aware of." She snapped her mouth shut. Knowing Malcolm had stashed away money didn't give her a strong motive for murder unless she'd also known he was broke.

"Since Malcolm has passed away, he'll also no longer be needing to stay in London on business. You have until the end of the month to vacate the flat."

Izzy growled and flew at Rhona. Biddy and I darted in between the two women. Izzy clawed at us to get to Rhona while Ava tried to remove the ring from the woman's finger. Two red nails snapped off, nearly hitting Biddy in an eye.

Dad tore Izzy away from us.

"Janey! You almost put my eye out."

Izzy gasped at the sight of her missing nails and stalked out of the room.

Biddy grabbed a cocktail napkin from the bar and dabbed at the blood on her temple.

"Are you all right?" Dad slipped onto the chair next to Rhona.

"Can't believe I let that woman get to me." She eased out a shaky breath. "Now I look like the jealous wife, despite having just learned about the affair."

According to Alec, Rhona had known about the affair. And how would she have known about Izzy living in the flat, unless she'd merely made the assumption?

"You have an alibi," Biddy told her.

Rhona nodded faintly, then took a gulp of tea. "You might as well know, since it's going to come out—I found out we were broke the afternoon before Malcolm's death. When I informed him I was investing in the castle with or without his approval, he told me good luck since we had no money to invest. I told him I was contacting a divorce solicitor and selling the house."

Ava's eyes widened. "You're selling our family home?"

"I'm putting it on the market to determine its value, but I would never sell it without the family's approval. I can't stay there. Too many bad memories."

Ava placed a comforting hand on Rhona's. "I understand. We'll figure it all out."

We left Dad to console Rhona while we went to find Tavish and tend to Biddy's wound.

"I wonder if Tavish or Ian told Rhona about Garrett and Malcolm's history," I said. "Not that I'm going to be the one to mention it. If any family member had known about Garrett, I'm sure it would have come out during Detective Henderson's questioning."

"I still just can't imagine that Malcolm wouldn't have gone off on Rhona for booking the hotel where his archenemy worked. No way could he have kept his anger in check, even if she'd unknowingly booked it."

"Unless he had a very good reason to keep quiet. Like maybe he knew before he got here that Garrett was the archer. He'd devised a scheme to steal the arrow and frame Garrett. Get the man thrown in jail like he should have been years ago for stealing Malcolm's prized bow."

Biddy's forehead crinkled. "Then Garrett would have to have stolen the arrow from Malcolm to shoot him with it. I think *Garrett* stole it to frame *Malcolm*. Revenge for filing charges against him and causing a scandal in their archery club. And Charlotte was in on it. That's why she freaked out and wanted to pull the arrow from the man's chest. Their plan to sell it was blown. Loads of money down the drain."

I nodded. "So not only was it about the money but also revenge. Kill two birds with one stone."

At some point the plan backfired and killed Malcolm.

Twelve

ON THE WAY down from our room after caring for Biddy's wound, we spied Izzy ahead of us on the staircase. Dressed in workout clothes, she was carrying a purple yoga mat. Now that she no longer had the means to pay for a massage, she'd have to rely on yoga to relieve her stress. She marched down the steps while we slowed our pace, keeping our distance. I did some yoga breathing.

Biddy touched the Snoopy bandage on her temple. She was a fun pediatric nurse. "And to think I was starting to feel bad for that woman even though she was getting on with a married man. She seemed to honestly love him."

I nodded. "I hate to admit it, but I feel a bit bad for her."

We reached the lobby and spotted Tavish through the open front door, lighting a cigarette by the fountain. We bolted outside as Izzy disappeared around the corner of the castle, heading toward the back garden.

"What's with Izzy?" Tavish asked. "She didn't even stop to rip me to shreds." He eyed Biddy's bandage. "Have a run-in with Woodstock, did ye?"

"Your ex-wife sliced my face with her bloody nails and nearly took an eye out."

Tavish cringed. "Her nails should be registered as a lethal weapon, as well as her tongue. Never won an argument with the lassie."

"We can discuss the catfight later," I said. "We have more important things to talk about." I filled Tavish in on my conversation with Detective Henderson and our encounter with Garrett while shopping in Dalwade. Ian hadn't told him about my call with the detective.

The man's cheeks burned as bright as his cigarette end. "It's time to have a talk with the bloke. If Garrett wants to blame someone, it should be me. And if he's blaming someone for merely telling the truth, then he has something to hide." He stubbed out a nearly full cigarette in the sand-filled urn.

Alec came flying up the drive in his small gray car. He hopped out of the vehicle without any deliveries. He smiled at Tavish rather than Biddy and me.

"Unhappy with the McAllister place, were ye?" he asked Tavish.

Tavish wore a tight smile. "Nay, it was braw. As was the takeaway."

"Told ye it's the best Indian food outside of Edinburgh."

Alec continued on inside.

I quirked a curious brow. When had Tavish stayed at the McAllister place?

"I arrived in town late the night Malcolm was killed. Was planning to meet with Ian and Ava about investing in this place. Suppose it looks bad I claimed to have flown in that morning. I came here but didn't feel up to a family gathering.

Was wrecked. Ended up not sleeping since Ian rang me about Malcolm."

If Tavish lied about not having been in town the night of the murder, had he also been in town when the arrow was stolen? Would he have risked being seen to steal it?

"Malcolm having an affair with my wife made me look guilty enough."

"How long had they been seeing each other?" I asked.

He shrugged. "I filed for divorce the day I found out six months ago when I caught them in our bed." His gaze darkened, peering off in the distance. The scene of his wife and brother in bed was likely burned into his memory forever. He lit up another cigarette. "I'll ring the detective straightaway, then pay Garrett Maxwell a visit." He stalked around the corner of the castle toward the archery course.

It started drizzling. The cool raindrops felt refreshing.

"He wouldn't have pointed the finger at Garrett to distract from the fact he'd lied about being in town, would he?" I said.

Biddy shook her head. "Absolutely not."

"Still, there's something fishy about Tavish not admitting he was in town the night Malcolm was murdered. I can't imagine he did it. But what if he'd known that Garrett is the hotel's archery instructor before he came here? Either Ava or Rhona might have mentioned his name, or maybe it's on the website. Either way, the family plot to kill their nasty sibling might have begun to brew. Maybe *three* people share the number-one suspect spot."

"Yet why would Rhona, Ava, Ian, or Tavish have stolen the arrow when they planned on investing in the hotel? The arrow was an important part of the castle's history."

"Because they knew as investors they'd look more innocent. Or they'd planned to frame Malcolm so he'd go to prison and Rhona would be free. Maybe they'd stolen it planning to use the money toward their investment. Maybe Archie was in on it."

My mind was reeling!

"I think we should check on Tavish and Garrett," I said.

Arguing carried out the front door from inside the castle. Lily and Alec.

"You'd think those two were married," I said.

Biddy and I headed inside to the registration area.

Lily glared at Alec. "He offered me twenty quid to tell him what room a guest is staying in. As if I can be bought."

The guy shrugged. "Sorry. Was merely offering ye part of what the shop owner paid me to collect the packages."

"Is this about Izzy Murray?" I asked.

He nodded. "She's supposed to be returning items to Chloe's."

"It's against policy to give out guests' rooms," Lily said.

"It's not against *my* policy," Biddy said. "She's in the Prince Albert Suite on the fourth floor."

Lily glared at Biddy, then Alec. "Remember, you didn't hear that from me."

Drenched, Izzy stalked through the front entrance with her rolled-up yoga mat. The drizzling had apparently turned into a downpour. She marched up the stairs.

Alec turned to us with an apprehensive look. "Might ye be able to go up with me? This could be worse than the bloke refusing to pay for his takeaway order last week."

Biddy touched her bandage. "We'd love to be helping ya repossess that woman's purchases."

A door slammed upstairs.

I flinched. "Maybe give her just a few minutes to calm down."

We took our time hiking up the sweeping staircase.

"So you made a delivery to Tavish when he was staying at the McAllister's?" I asked.

"From Ginger's Curry, an Indian restaurant. He was lucky he placed the order just before the kitchen closed."

"What time do they close?"

"Eight on Tuesdays."

Tavish had been in town prior to Malcolm's murder. He could have polished off his chicken curry in plenty of time to head over here and kill his brother.

We arrived at Izzy's room, and I rapped on the door. After several moments, footsteps approached. I could feel her glare through the peephole.

"Go away!" she yelled.

"You owe me an apology," Biddy said. "I demand you open this door right now."

"Go...away."

"Izzy, please open the door," I said. "It's important."

We stared at the door until Izzy slowly opened it, wearing the white spa robe over her wet clothes. Flames danced in the fireplace behind her.

She spied Alec standing there, and her lips pursed. "Fine." She marched over to the unopened packages on the bench at the foot of the bed. She whipped a small box across the room. We ducked as it flew into the hallway.

"I'm just doing my job." Alec snatched up the box.

Izzy collapsed onto the bed. "Sorry. Take them. Take them all." She swept a dramatic arm toward the lovely pink bags and boxes. "I have nothing left. Not even a place to live."

We helped Alec carry the packages into the hall.

Before closing the door, I looked in at Izzy sobbing on the bed. "We can't leave her like this."

"Most certainly can," Biddy said.

"The woman's a wreck. Besides, I want to ask her a few questions."

Biddy let out a defeated sigh. "Fine."

We loaded Alec up with packages for the first trip to his car, then closed the door and joined Izzy.

"If Malcolm stashed money at your flat and the police find it, you're going to look guilty of his murder, especially if you knew he was broke."

"If he'd hidden money, he wouldn't have confided in me about it. Money was his one true love he'd have done anything for."

Including getting himself murdered?

Shivering, Izzy stood and tightened the sash on her robe. "Sorry about your face," she told Biddy.

Biddy nodded, touching her bandage.

Izzy dropped down onto the couch near the fire, and we sat on the love seat across from her. Melting, I stripped off my Scotland sweatshirt.

"I'm heading back to London tomorrow." She grabbed a pillow and hugged it against her front. "Need to find a place to live. The only reason I'm still here is because I want to help the police find Malcolm's killer. To find the person who ruined my future and chance at happiness." Her cheeks reddened.

"Did Malcolm mention he'd known Garrett Maxwell from years ago?" I asked.

Izzy's perfectly arched eyebrows furrowed. "Who's Garrett Maxwell?"

"The archer," I said.

"Oh yeah. No, Malcolm never mentioned that."

"They belonged to the same archery club. Didn't get along."

Izzy's eyes widened. "You think he murdered Malcolm?"

"No, I'm not saying that. Was just curious if Malcolm had mentioned him."

If Malcolm had been going to confide in anyone about his history with Garrett, I'd have thought it would be Izzy.

"That would make sense." Izzy nodded slowly. "Malcolm hung around after the archery competition, talking to Garrett. I thought maybe he was apologizing for breaking the arrow, but it was turning into a lengthy conversation, so I left." Izzy shook her head. "Maybe he was in on it with Ava."

"Ava?" Biddy said.

"She despised Malcolm more than anyone. She definitely took her best friend's side in that marriage. When he refused to invest in this hotel, she threatened him."

"About what?" I asked.

Izzy shrugged. "He wouldn't discuss it. Just came storming to my suite about Ava threatening him, telling him he was going to be sorry. I'd never seen him so angry."

Had Ava told him he was possibly...my father, which had made him furious? No way could the man have been any more upset about the discovery than I had!

🍀 🍀

Watching our backs and fronts, Biddy and I peeked around every corner on the lookout for Garrett as we headed down four flights of stairs. He was likely on the prowl for us after his conversation with Tavish.

"How are we going to prove the man's guilty when we're doing everything we can to avoid him?" Biddy said.

"Speaking of avoiding, why isn't he allowing the police to question his wife? Because she knows he's guilty? I wonder if anyone has seen her since the murder. What if he's done something more sinister than keeping her heavily sedated? He can't afford to kill her, or he'd look even more suspicious."

"Unless he made it look like suicide and planted evidence to frame her for the murder. Someone needs to check on Charlotte."

We popped by the registration desk.

Lily gave Biddy the evil eye.

"I'm not sorry for telling him Izzy's room," Biddy said. "The woman made all those purchases with a dead man's credit card. His wife shouldn't have to pay for them."

Lily's gaze softened. "Suppose not."

"Have you seen Charlotte around?" I asked her.

"Nay, I haven't." She glanced at a clipboard on her desk. "Garrett's giving a lesson in fifteen minutes. Maybe she'll be down at the course."

We thanked Lily and headed out the front door. We rounded the castle's corner, and shouting carried up the hill from the archery grounds. Biddy and I hit the deck and peered below at Tavish and Garrett in each other's face. I snapped a quick pic in case anything happened to Tavish and we needed evidence. Yet if it turned into a brawl, my money was on Tavish. Nowhere to hide, we took advantage of Garrett being occupied and raced toward his cottage to check on his wife. Only his blue BMW sat in the gravel drive in front of the small stone cottage with a yellow door and matching trimmed windows.

"I can't imagine Charlotte doesn't have a vehicle," I said. "And there isn't a garage."

Biddy rapped on the door. No answer. We skulked around the house, peeking in windows.

"We'll have to ask Lily about a second car," I said.

Loud banging came from a stone shed outside the garden's shrub fence. Biddy and I exchanged curious glances. We approached the shed, where someone was cussing up a storm inside. We peeked through the open door at Archie surrounded by some rather medieval-looking garden tools, lawn equipment, and shelves packed with weed killer, plant food, and other supplies. Several rusted signs on the walls advertised Scotch, plant seeds, and companies that had likely gone out of business a century ago.

"Is everything okay?" I asked Archie.

He forced a smile. "Yes indeed, all is well. An animal must have gotten in."

I eyed the broken glass on the shed's floor and the open window. Pretty smart animal to open a window.

Archie slipped the white hankie from his blazer pocket and wiped his forehead and pale cheeks. His breathing became labored, and he braced a hand against the stone wall.

"You don't look good." I stepped inside the shed, immersed in the smell of grease, grime, and grass clippings.

Biddy and I helped the man take a seat on a run-down green riding lawn mower. A grease spot on Archie's blue suede shoe about sent him over the edge. Biddy grabbed a pair of large gloves and started fanning him.

"Someone has broken into the shed," he said. "I called the gardener to come see if anything was stolen." He patted his forehead. "I don't wish to call the police, even if something was taken. One theft and a murder could happen anywhere. But *two* thefts, and people will believe it isn't safe to stay here."

I'd already questioned how safe the place was before someone might have stolen a spade, pruner, or other lethal weapon from the shed.

"We had a string of shed break-ins back home," Biddy said. "The guards caught the thieves, who had a building filled with nicked lawn tractors and power tools. You'd think a thief would have nicked your tractor if anything."

The ancient mower, along with the rest of the shed's contents, would be a dream come true for the guys from the reality show *Hicking and Picking*. Not for a professional lawn thief. The thief had likely broken in, decided it wasn't worth risking jail time, then fled.

"Was possibly kids drinking a few beers, hanging out at a murder scene so they could brag to their buddies." Someone like Alec and his friends.

Archie lowered his hankie from his forehead, nodding. "You're probably spot on. The gardener sometimes finds discarded beer cans and wrappers in here. Before the door's rusted latch was replaced, the window was kept unlocked in case the door wouldn't open. Might be best off fixing the window and leaving it unlocked once again to prevent more broken windows."

The owner seemed in better spirits, no longer on the

verge of a stroke, so Biddy and I headed toward the archery course. Tavish was gone, and Garrett was giving a lesson to an older man. We found Tavish stalking back and forth in the front drive.

He took a long drag on his cigarette and eased out the smoke, trying to calm down from his confrontation. "The man claims if he was going to off Malcolm, he'd have done it twenty years ago. Not now when he has it made here."

"Maybe seeing Malcolm brought back bad memories, and Garrett had wanted revenge once and for all," I said.

Tavish nodded, extinguishing a half cigarette. "Malcolm certainly brought out the worst in people."

"Garrett would have known about the security cameras not working in the garden or corridor," I said. "He also likely had access to the offices and could have found the display case's key. We could bluff and claim we knew Malcolm had discovered Garrett stole the arrow and that I'd heard them arguing about it an hour before he was found dead. Maybe Garrett would get angry and confess."

Tavish's jaw tightened. "Stay away from the man and let the police handle it. You lassies should be enjoying what's left of your holiday."

Enjoy our holiday? Was he serious?

I told him about our concern over Izzy's mental state.

"Believe me, Izzy is far from fragile," Tavish said. "But I'll see how she's getting on—if she'll even open the door for me. Before talking with Garrett, I rang Detective Henderson and filled him in on more details about Malcolm and Garrett's past. Also about me having been in town the night of my brother's murder. Will forward him my flight itinerary proving I was out of the country when the arrow was nicked.

If for no other reason, I wouldn't have killed Malcolm for the sake of our mother's memory—the only woman Malcolm ever respected."

Ian had made a similar comment about his mother. It seemed there was some resentment about how the black sheep of the family had been their mother's favorite.

"He was her cross to bear. She blamed herself for the way he turned out. But Malcolm was never wired right."

"Like not going to his grandmother's funeral?"

He nodded. "Aye. Ava must have mentioned that to you. She never let him live it down. And was upset with Ian and me for not forcing him on the bloody plane."

The hairs stood straight on the back of my neck. "You and Ian were in Chicago with him when your grandma Murray died?"

Biddy went rigid next to me.

"Aye. Ian's wife had died a few months before. He was a wreck. Needed to get away. Surprisingly, it was Malcolm who'd recommended the trip. One of the few times the man showed any compassion for others. Our father and your grandfather had stayed in touch and visited back and forth every few years. We thought it would be nice to meet your family."

When I'd spoken to Ian about his grandma's funeral, why hadn't he mentioned having been in Chicago? Because he'd figured out their visit had been approximately nine months prior to my birth and that Malcolm might have been my father?

Or that *Ian* himself might be my father?

Even if he didn't know my age or the year his grandmother died, he might have realized the two incidents had taken place around the same time.

Why hadn't Ava mentioned her other two brothers had been in Chicago at that time? An innocent slip of her mind, or intentional? Proving all three had been there would make Dad look less guilty. He wouldn't have planned to randomly kill the brothers off one at a time, unsure which was my biological father.

Out of the corner of my eye, I saw the three elderly aunts exiting the castle, dragging their luggage behind them. We all flew over to assist them.

"Leaving already, aunties?" Tavish said.

Fenella nodded. "Aye, need to be getting back home to Ross. Man can't even heat a can of soup for himself. And best start preparing for the funeral. Doesn't sound like Rhona will be holding a wake." She shook her head. "What a shame."

"Might you change her mind?" the woman with the pink cane asked Tavish.

He smiled. "Will see what I can do."

"Especially since a bit of a damper was put on the gathering, would be lovely to have a proper get-together. I could be making a nice Scotch pie."

Tavish smiled. "Sounds delicious."

"Can't have a funeral without cock-a-leekie soup," the woman with the brown wig added.

He gave her a wink. "Most certainly can't."

A taxi pulled up the drive.

"Let me take you young lassies to the train station," Tavish said.

"Don't be silly, pet. Our ride is here." She gave Tavish a

kiss on the cheek. "You've always been such a dear. You and Ian both."

Not Malcolm.

Tavish loaded the suitcases into the taxi's trunk, and we hugged the women goodbye. I mentally crossed them off our suspect list, unable to picture the women committing such a violent murder. Now, if Malcolm had been standing in the drive, I could possibly imagine the one aunt running him down in the heat of the moment. Revenge for having run over her poor cat.

"Ah, there you two are," Dad said, walking out the front door. "Was about to head to the cemetery looking for you."

"Speaking of which," Tavish said. "I was wondering if Mags might fancy giving me a tour of the graveyard."

I plastered on a smile. "Sure. We also have to fit in a tour of the secret passageway before we leave."

Biddy snapped her fingers. "Ah, shoot, won't be able to join ya in the graveyard. Have a spa appointment. Must crack on or will be late for it."

"I'll go with you. Need to grab my aluminum foil."

We fled inside, leaving Dad and Tavish standing there.

My heart raced as we marched up the staircase. "You know what this means?"

"It's like *Mama Mia* all over again when the girl invites her three potential fathers to her wedding in Greece to determine which one it is."

"Yeah, except none of them were murdered."

"I'd rather be the daughter of a possible murderer than Malcolm."

Funny how everything was relative. In this case, hopefully *not* a relative when it came to murder.

Thirteen

DAD, Tavish, Ian, and I walked through the garden toward the cemetery. The men were discussing a possible golf outing next summer at Scotland's top courses. Hopefully, they wouldn't have to prepay greens fees. Either Ian or Tavish, or possibly both, might be in prison. Even if they weren't, the men likely wouldn't be on such friendly terms with Dad if one of them turned out to be my biological father.

Would they still be on friendly terms with *me*?

As much as I despised Malcolm, I was starting to hope maybe he would turn out to be my father. I hated to damage Ian's and Tavish's relationship with Dad or me. I really liked both men—unless one had a heated night of passion with my mother.

What if it hadn't merely been one night?

Heat rose up my neck and burned on my cheeks. I wanted to flee to my guest room. Yet if I did, Dad might be wrongly accused of murder.

We walked over the stone bridge and headed through the cemetery's gate. The calming scent of lush foliage, moss, and damp earth relieved the tension in my body better and cheaper than a trip to the hotel's spa.

"Have fond memories of the graveyard near where we grew up." Tavish wore a mischievous grin. "Was where I shared my first kiss with Katie McFarlane."

Ian quirked a brow. "Took her there under the pretense it was haunted, eh? So she'd get scared and stay close for protection."

"Aye, same reason you gave Olivia Patterson, I suppose."

Ian wore a guilty grin. "How 'bout yourself?" he asked Dad.

"Grew up in the Chicago area. Would have been risking both our lives sneaking around a cemetery at night."

"Can't say I've ever kissed a guy in an Ireland cemetery either," I said.

Tavish leaned over and kissed me on the cheek. "Now you can say a guy kissed you in a Scotland graveyard."

A guy who might be my father.

My cheek burned where he'd placed the kiss.

"Tell us about your plans for the restoration project," Ian said.

I excitedly described my Adopt-a-Grave idea and a Facebook page to spark local interest in maintaining the cemetery.

I took them over to Lady Kerr's scratched tombstone. "Volunteers will be taught how to clean and care for headstones. This will prevent people from using harsh chemicals or steel wool to remove moss and lichen, damaging the stones in the process. Any illegible stones will have a plaque with the grave's information."

"What about a map at the entrance detailing the layout of the graveyard?" Tavish said.

Ian gave his brother a pat on the back. "Some world adventurer you are. Should want to explore the graves, uncovering one stone at a time."

I smiled. "Exactly. However, a plaque by the church will provide its history along with the cemetery's. And a display holder will offer information pamphlets for a nominal donation."

"That's pure dead brilliant," Ian said. "A Scottish expression, not a reference to the residents here."

Dad smiled and slipped an arm around my shoulder. "She makes her dad proud."

I shifted my stance on the uneven ground, uneasy over the possibility that I was standing there with both my dads. "I assisted my grandma with a few restorations. It's not easy to reverse the effects of mother nature, neglect, and vandalism. We once spent half my summer vacation removing graffiti from graves."

Tavish shook his head. "Bloody shame people don't respect the dead."

"Mags recently came across a dead body—well, actually two, on her grandparents' graves," Dad said.

Ian's eyes widened. "Aye, did you? That must have been quite a scare."

"Despite my nicknames Shovel Slayer and Tombstone Terminator, I didn't kill the man."

I told them about how I'd solved the mystery of the person in the purple pouch and how it'd helped me trace Grandpa Fitzsimmons's line back to Michael Collins, who'd led Ireland's fight for independence against England.

Tavish looked impressed. "Fair play to ya. Being related to Ireland's greatest hero would certainly be worth having a few possible felons in the family line. I'm sure there isn't a line without skeletons in it."

Dad managed to hide any uneasiness over the man's comment, as hopefully I did also.

"Our Murrays trace back to Robert the Bruce," Ian said.

Wow. The man who'd freed Scotland from English rule was in my other family line. People paid genealogists big bucks to discover a gateway ancestor—a person in your family line who descended from royalty or nobility. I'd discovered two for free.

"You have to take the good with the bad," Tavish said. "Ava was five when her mother died, and she came to live with us. That was how our mum learned about our father's affair."

Last night when Ava had mentioned she didn't share the same mother as her siblings, I was more focused on her devastating news about Malcolm. Tavish wouldn't have shared a story about a skeleton in the Murray closet if he knew I was also a skeleton. Either he hadn't had an affair with Mom, or he hadn't a clue that I'd been the result of it.

Three of our lives were about to change forever, unless one of the three was already dead. If not, besides Dad and me, would the third life be Ian or Tavish?

☘ ☘

Following the cemetery tour, the men headed inside for a drink in the library while I hung back to regroup. The clock was ticking until Ava filled Detective Henderson in on our relationship and my possible connection with Malcolm. I had to find Charlotte. The woman was likely the key to proving her husband was a murderer.

Rhona wandered through the gate, talking on the phone, unaware of my presence. I made a mental note to add a sign at the entrance forbidding cell phone usage except for taking photos. The dead, as well as the living, should be allowed to rest in peace. I, for one, would like to.

Rhona finished the call and plucked a tissue from the pocket of her brown quilted jacket. She dropped down on a rotting bench I feared she'd fall through. I went over to her.

"Sienna is devasted over her father's death. Poor pet." She blew her nose. "Her flight back from Australia is delayed. She's so upset she's threatening to quit university, with only a semester left, to be closer to home. She'd gone to Australia to be far away from home, to have her freedom. I didn't argue about it, but there's no way she's quitting."

"I'm sure she won't quit. Her world was just turned upside down. She's not thinking straight."

"Malcolm would never have raised a quitter. Despite all his faults, he had more drive than any person I've ever known. He couldn't bear to fail at anything in life. Couldn't admit defeat. Thankfully, she inherited that trait from him."

"Were they close?"

"Closer than anyone was to him. He wasn't exactly a warm man."

That was putting it mildly.

"When my mom died four years ago, I was working at a vineyard in Napa. I quit and went straight home to be with my dad. I swore I was never leaving again. A month later he found me a job working at his friend's dude ranch in Montana. He insisted I take it. That my mom would have wanted me to. However, she'd never approved of me working seasonal jobs rather than going to college. Yet it was what my dad wanted, and I wanted him to be happy."

Rhona smiled. "I hope you're right and she doesn't do anything drastic and throw away a good education, like I did."

"If she does quit, she can always go back next semester."

"Lucky for me I possess many traits her father didn't. Like being frugal and planning for a rainy day. Malcolm might have been broke, but I'd put plenty of money aside over the years in my own account without him knowing. Enough to take care of myself and Sienna as well as investing in the castle."

That certainly decreased Rhona's motive to murder her husband for the insurance money. Besides, she wouldn't have left Sienna parentless.

"Is Detective Henderson aware of this?"

She nodded, checking the time on her phone. "I have to meet Ava for a drink, then pack. I keep meaning to ask if you and Biddy would each want an extra Queen Victoria china cup. You mentioned how much you liked them. I brought two additional in case any were broken when being delivered to rooms."

"We'd love them."

"You can collect them from my suite." She handed me her room key.

I smiled at the key, happy that Rhona obviously had nothing to hide if she was allowing me access to her room. However, I wasn't sure what evidence she'd have had to hide even if she was guilty of her husband's murder. Still, it made me optimistic that Rhona was innocent.

I hiked up the stairs toward the Queen Victoria Suite, trying to picture the queen having promenaded up and down five flights of stairs in those heavy dresses and undergarments. Maybe her room had actually been on the second floor in what was now a meeting room, but they'd named the fanciest suite after her. I encountered Biddy between the third and fourth floors. She was carefully navigating the carpeted steps in spa flip-flops, walking on her heels, her toes up in the air so her blue-and-green plaid nails wouldn't get smudged.

"Took over an hour to paint the bloody yokes." She blew on her short, perfectly rounded fingernails that matched her toes.

"You should have gotten fake nails in case you're in another cat fight with Izzy. At least you'd be on an even playing field."

Biddy went with me to Rhona's room to collect our bonus gift. I opened the suite's door and startled Lily rifling through desk drawers.

Panic flickered in the girl's blue eyes, yet she managed one of her perky smiles. "Oh, hi. Ah, I'm filling in as the porter, seeing as Charlie hasn't been replaced." She glanced around the room, her gaze landing on the beverage station. "Just brought more tea and biscuits."

I gave the open drawer a skeptical look.

Lily slammed the drawer shut. "The theft and murder were all my fault."

"Janey," Biddy muttered. "She wasn't even on our list of suspects. How'd we miss seeing that one coming?"

"Because"—I directed my reply to Lily rather than Biddy

—"she had an airtight alibi for the time of the murder, having been at the registration desk."

Lily's eyes widened. "I didn't mean I'd murdered the man. Even though I'd wanted to after I realized what he'd done."

"What had he done, and why are you in here?" I asked.

"I'm looking for the key to the arrow's display case."

"I didn't think the key was stolen," I said.

Lily frowned. "It was. I replaced it with the extra Archie apparently forgot he'd had me make."

"And you think Malcolm nicked the key?" Biddy said.

Lily nodded, sinking onto the couch. "I feel like a total gobshite. He claimed he was going to be a major investor in the hotel and thought I'd make a brilliant manager. That I likely knew the running of the place better than anyone except Archie. He said Archie should spend more time growing the business than overseeing the day-to-day operations of the hotel. I told him that'd be fab. That I loved my job but was worried that the hotel would close because Archie couldn't even afford security cameras."

"Malcolm knew the cameras weren't working?" I sat on the love seat across from Lily, and Biddy joined me.

"He questioned if the valuable items in the corridor were secure, and I foolishly admitted they weren't. I also mentioned neither were the keys in Archie's desk drawer. Why didn't I keep my gob shut?"

"You're not the first woman to fall prey to the man's charm," Biddy said.

"I need to replace the key before Archie remembers the extra. I can't get sacked over this."

"Lily," I said. "You're going to have to tell Archie and the detective what you think happened."

"I *know* it happened." She twirled a clump of blond hair nervously around a finger. "When I was showing Mr. Murray the back offices, he became a bit...overly friendly with me. I didn't know what to do since he was talking about making me manager. Thankfully, the bloody phone started ringing out front, so I went to answer it. Nobody was there. I think he autodialed it on his mobile to get me out of the office. He walked out from the back and left without saying a word. After the theft, I knew he'd taken the key. Yet if I accused him, I'd have to admit my involvement and chance getting sacked. Or worse yet, he might have blamed me for the theft and I'd have ended up in prison." Her eyes watered, and her bottom lip trembled.

No wonder the poor girl had been such a total wreck.

"If Malcolm had the key, that means he had the arrow," Biddy said. "That will look really bad for Rhona."

"What if the arrow was what Garrett and Malcolm's argument was about? Garrett knew Malcolm had stolen it, and when Malcolm refused to give him a cut, Garrett stole the arrow from his room." I looked at Lily. "Could he have had access to the guest room keys?"

"Aye. An extra key for each room is hanging in the back office."

"Maybe once Malcolm discovered Garrett was the archery instructor, he put the plan into action to frame him for the theft. Yet he never had the opportunity to do so."

I nodded. "We really need to talk to Charlotte." I turned to Lily. "Have you seen her around?"

Lily shook her head. "Nay. You think she was in on it with Garrett?"

"In on what?" Rhona demanded, entering the room.

We all sprang up from our seats.

She eyed Lily. "What are you doing in here?"

Lily paled. "Ah, I, was, er..."

I explained Lily's reason for believing Malcolm had stolen the arrow.

"So if my husband stole the arrow, I must have killed him? Is that what you think?"

We all shook our heads.

"Search the suite." Rhona swept an arm through the air. "I have nothing to hide."

We followed Rhona into the bedroom, where she dumped the contents of the nightstand drawers onto the bed. Antacids, earplugs, eyeshades, and other common items found in a nightstand. She pulled a suitcase from the closet and started tossing out dirty clothes. A key flew from the pocket of a pair of navy slacks. The pants Malcolm had worn to the reception.

"That's the key," Lily muttered.

We stood there staring at the key on the red-and-gold patterned carpet.

Archie flew into the room, trying to catch his breath from having run up the stairs. "What's...going on...here?" Patting his forehead with his white hankie, he peered over at Lily. "Been looking everywhere for you. What are you doing leaving the desk unattended?" When Lily didn't respond, his gaze darted to the key on the floor. He snatched it up. "What is this key for?"

I brought Archie up to speed on Lily's theory about Malcolm having stolen the arrow.

Lily grimaced. "I know I should have told you."

Archie patted his brow. "Indeed. We all make mistakes, but you should have told me about Malcolm and the theft. More importantly, you should have told the police. Withholding information is obstructing an investigation." Archie pressed both hands down the front of his wrinkled blazer.

Lily fought back tears. "Am I going to prison?"

"No, I'm sure that's not the case," I told her.

She gestured to Rhona. "She wasn't with Ava Murray the night of the murder. I saw the women coming from different directions a few minutes after each other."

"It's true," Rhona said. "I should have admitted straightaway that I'd been in my room alone. However, I knew how bad it looked. Nobody had more reasons than I did for wanting Malcolm dead. Ava realized that and feared I'd be at the top of the suspect list, so she claimed we were together. I didn't say otherwise." Rhona massaged her forearm. It probably needed ointment for her fibromyalgia. "What a bloody mess."

I shook my head. "If you'd discovered the arrow and used it to kill your husband, you wouldn't have just tossed the room, claiming the key wasn't here. That'd make no sense."

"If Malcolm had the key, the arrow must have been here at some point for Garrett to have nicked it," Biddy said.

Rhona shrugged. "He might have had it hidden here. The suite is huge."

"Hold on," Archie said. "Garrett *Maxwell* stole the arrow and killed the man?"

I held up a halting hand. "It's merely a theory. I

shouldn't have shared it without more evidence. That can't leave this room." I filled Archie in on Malcolm and Garrett's past. "Charlotte likely holds the answer as to what happened, since it's awfully fishy that she's disappeared in the middle of a murder investigation. Particularly when she's the one who found the body."

"She checked herself into a mental health facility," Archie said. "Wasn't doing well after the murder."

Thankfully, Garrett hadn't offed his wife. Regardless, the woman knew something.

"I have to tell the police everything." Lily snatched her phone from her blazer pocket. "I'm ringing Detective Henderson."

"Now wait a moment," Archie said. "Let's think this through. Maybe there's no reason to ring the police."

Was he more worried about his biggest investor going to prison or a scandal involving the hotel's famous archer?

"No, you need to tell them what you know, luv." Rhona gave Lily an encouraging smile. "That's precisely what I'd advise Sienna to do. I won't have you getting in trouble for something Malcolm did. I swear I'm innocent of my husband's murder."

"She most certainly is." Ian stood in the doorway. "Because *I* murdered my brother."

Rhona peered at Ian in horror. "Don't say such a ridiculous thing, Ian. I truly am innocent. I know the entire family suspects I did it, but everyone can stop trying to protect me. I didn't kill Malcolm."

"I'm not protecting you. I killed my brother."

"Stop it!" Rhona demanded. "Don't do this just because we—"

"Don't say another word." I glanced between the couple, not wanting them to profess their love for each other in front of a group of witnesses. Giving them both another, even stronger, motive for murder. "Think about what you're doing."

Ian gave me a pointed look. "I know what I'm doing. I'm not allowing anyone else to go to jail for what I did."

Instead of proving Dad wasn't a murderer, would I now have to prove my possible biological father wasn't one?

Unless Ian really was guilty.

Fourteen

WHILE WAITING for the police to arrive, Dad, Ava, and Tavish joined us in the boardroom off the lobby. Ava was consoling Rhona, who sobbed uncontrollably while Tavish insisted that Ian retract his statement.

Tavish raked a frustrated hand through his thick salt-and-pepper hair. "Ian, think about what you're doing. This is bloody insane. Can't be confessing to a murder ye didn't commit."

Ian stared blankly at the massive wood table, done discussing the matter.

Tavish slammed a fist on the table in front of his brother, who didn't even flinch. "Damnit. I refuse to be losing you because of Malcolm. Don't do this!"

Detective Henderson entered the room with two uniformed officers.

Rhona flew to the detective. "Ian didn't do it. He's only confessing because he thinks I did it."

The detective's gaze narrowed on Rhona. "Did ye?"

She shook her head. "No, but neither did he."

The detective peered down at Ian, still seated at the table. "You're aware that confessing to a crime ye didn't commit is a crime in itself?"

Ian nodded. "Why would I confess if I'm not guilty?"

The detective shrugged. "Don't know why anyone would be mad enough to give a false confession, but they do. For money, drugs, many reasons."

"Well, I'm not."

An officer read Ian his rights while slapping the cuffs on his wrists. Rhona let out a distressed cry. Tavish slipped an arm around her shoulder, and she wilted against his broad chest, sobbing. The police led Ian outside, and I trailed behind, my heart racing.

"Wait," I said when they reached the police vehicle. "Can I have a quick word with him?"

Detective Henderson told the two officers to give us a moment.

"Are you my father?" I blurted out.

Ian appeared taken aback.

"I have DNA evidence that one of you brothers is."

Ian peered into my eyes for what seemed like forever, as if trying to determine if they were the same shade of blue as his, with his same thick lashes. Finally, he nodded. "Aye."

A sense of relief washed over me that Malcolm wasn't my biological father. Relief quickly evolved into anger that I'd finally identified my father when he was being handcuffed and arrested for murder.

"How long have you known?" I demanded.

"About a minute. I'm sorry." He shook his head with regret. Regret over the affair with my mother or having falsely confessed to a murder before realizing he had a daughter?

Yet what if it wasn't a false confession?

And what if Ian had known I was his daughter? Maybe that was the reason he'd always been so sweet to me. Playing cards with me rather than poker with the men. Buying me the Lady Mags Murray T-shirt, and the land and title had likely been his idea. Even if he hadn't known for sure, had he always suspected he was my biological father?

Ian frowned, sliding onto the back seat of the police car.

A part of me wished Malcolm had been my father. He was a much easier man to hate.

My entire body trembling, I turned to find Dad standing there, shell-shocked. "How long have you suspected Ian was your biological father?"

I told him about Ava's visit to my room the night before. "I hadn't been in my account in weeks. I didn't have a clue. I knew there was no way you'd murdered Malcolm, but what if the police didn't agree? I needed to find the killer to prove your innocence."

Dad shook his head in disbelief. "You should have told me what was going on, Mags."

"Finding the killer was a priority over finding my biological father. I couldn't turn the focus of the investigation on us until I had answers. I'm sorry this is how you had to find out. Please don't be upset."

An incredulous look furrowed Dad's brow. "Don't worry about me. I'm worried about you."

"I'm fine," I assured him.

He gave me a skeptical look and wrapped me in his arms.

I burst into tears.

I was closer to solving this puzzling mystery than I was to being fine.

Sitting on the blue-and-gold upholstered couch in Dad's room, I choked down Scotch from his Queen Victoria china cup. Dad was seated on a matching chair across from me by the fireplace, sipping Scotch from a crystal glass. At least we weren't drinking straight from the Clan Murray souvenir bottle like I had last night.

I eyed the open suitcase on the four-poster bed's red duvet, where clean shirts were neatly folded in plastic dry cleaner bags. "I've had my fill of Scotland. Let's skip our stay in Edinburgh and head to Ireland. We can hang out at my place and McCarthy's pub the rest of your trip."

"This isn't something you can run away from, Mags."

"I'm not trying to run away. Not like I can have a relationship with a man doing life in prison."

"Do you believe he deserves life in prison?"

I nodded. "That's what you get for killing a man."

My uncle.

I dropped back against the couch. "I really thought Garrett Maxwell was guilty."

Dad gave me a pointed look. "Is that what you still think?"

I fessed up about Biddy's and my encounter with the archer in Dalwade. "And don't scold me for putting my life in danger. That's precisely why I didn't tell you what I was doing. And I had to figure out the killer before you were blamed."

"Fine. I won't scold you for putting your life in jeopardy, but—"

"No buts, Dad. Tavish had our backs, and Detective

Henderson was aware of Garrett and Malcolm's past. However, I'm sure he's not going to continue looking into Garrett now that Ian has confessed. Garrett is off the hook and has gotten away with murder."

"You *don't* believe Ian is guilty."

"Doesn't matter what I believe. I'm done investigating. Don't worry." I gagged down another gulp of Scotch. "I can't believe how well you're taking all of this."

Dad stared into his Scotch. "Oh, I'm upset as hell about what happened between your mother and Ian." His grip tightened on the crystal glass. "I could whip this glass into the fireplace and storm around, but that wouldn't change what happened twenty-eight years ago. And it won't help either of us right now."

Maybe not, yet if I wasn't drinking from the coveted Queen Victoria teacup, hurling the china into the fireplace sounded like a great stress reliever.

Dad set his glass on the table. "I can't believe I never had a clue. I was certain the men's first visit was two years before you were born, when Emma was a year old rather than two. I was oblivious and partly responsible for what happened."

"That's ridiculous. How can you say that?"

"I was her husband and didn't realize how unhappy she apparently was. Unhappy enough to turn to another man. I was traveling too much for my job at that time to even realize what was happening at home." He pinched the bridge of his nose, undoubtedly experiencing a whopper of a headache, like I was. "Was she unhappy our entire marriage?"

"Ian was the only other man, and don't wonder otherwise. And don't you dare blame yourself. Despite traveling, you were around more than she was. Even if she was unhappy, that doesn't justify what she did."

I had to believe that Ian had been the only man and their relationship had merely been a one-night fling, not a yearlong thing.

"We need to forgive them both," Dad said. "Not for their sakes—for ours. If I'd learned about the affair at the time it happened, I would have forgiven your mother. I loved her. I wouldn't have thrown away our marriage."

"Even if I can somehow forgive him, that doesn't mean we'll have a relationship." Granted, if it hadn't been for Ian, I wouldn't be alive and sitting here right now with Dad, trying to forgive the man. Talk about a double-edged sword.

A rap sounded on the door. Likely Biddy checking on me.

Dad opened the door to find Rhona. Her eyes were puffy, her cheeks red and blotchy. She entered the room, along with the smell of menthol, and thoughts of Grandpa Murray once again filled my head. Ian going to jail must have caused her fibromyalgia to flare up. Dad escorted her over to a chair.

She peered at me through a glassy-eyed haze. "I wasn't aware of Ian's relationship with your mother." She turned to Dad. "Not sure if you recall that his visit to Chicago was after the recent loss of his wife. He was only twenty-four."

My gaze narrowed on Rhona. "That's awful he lost his wife, but it doesn't justify what he did to our family."

"Mags," Dad said calmly, flipping on the tea kettle switch.

The kettle hissed to life.

I dropped back onto the couch.

"I can't even imagine what you are going through." Rhona's voice filled with emotion. "Losing Ian now that I have the chance to be happy and with the man I love would be unbearable." She stared into the fireplace, a lost look on her face. "Maybe if you go and see him, you can get him to retract his statement."

A knock sounded on the door.

Dad handed Rhona a cup of tea and answered the door.

Archie marched in, hankie in hand. "I want to know more about Garrett Maxwell having possibly stolen the arrow. This is quite disturbing, to say the least."

"It's just a theory," I said.

"Prove your theory that Garrett Maxwell is guilty." Archie patted his forehead with the hankie. "You must be right. It makes perfect sense. If you don't, I have no choice but to confront the man. I can't have an untrustworthy employee."

I sprang from the couch. "If you do that, he'll know it was me who told you."

Archie's shoulders drooped. "He mustn't get away with this. Even if he didn't kill Malcolm, the man can't continue working here if he had anything to do with stealing the arrow." He perked up. "How about a five-thousand-pound reward for determining Garrett's involvement, if any at all?"

Rhona surged to her feet. "I'll contribute another five to prove he murdered Malcolm and Ian is innocent."

My head was spinning.

"How about you give Mags a bit of time to consider your offers," Dad said. "I think she's overwhelmed with everything going on right now."

Rhona gave me a sympathetic smile. "Of course you are,

luv. I appreciate whatever you can do, and let me know if I can help in any way." She gave me a hug before leaving.

Archie agreed to hold off confronting Garrett until I responded to the offer and was a safe distance from the archer.

He left, and Dad and I sat sipping Scotch in silence.

"If I decide to help them, I'm certainly not taking any money for it."

Dad nodded in agreement. "I think you've already made a decision, haven't you?"

I stared into my drink. "Yeah, I guess I have. We should stick around a bit, then go to Edinburgh."

I went back to my room and told Biddy about Archie and Rhona's visit.

"I agree. We need to get Ian out of jail," Biddy said. "It isn't right. It's sad, yet how utterly romantic having a man who would take a murder rap for you." She plopped onto her bed, with a wistful look. "I doubt Collin would."

"You've only been dating a few months. I think it's a bit soon to be expecting the guy to go to prison for you."

"Wouldn't it be best to know early on if a relationship is worth pursuing?"

"It could take a few years for you to get to that point. Would *you* go to prison for *him*?"

"That's not the same."

"Why not?"

"It's the hero who always goes to prison for the heroine."

"That's sexist."

"That's Hollywood." She grabbed her phone off the nightstand. "I need to be ringing him anyway. Haven't spoken to him since we arrived." Biddy put the call on speakerphone, and Collin answered. "No phone sex. Mags is here with me."

"Hey, Mags, how's the craic?" Collin sounded his usual upbeat self. That was likely about to change.

"It's grand," Biddy said. "Except for a murder. A nasty fella, yet still put a bit of a damper on our holiday. Anyway, hypothetically, if I committed a crime and might possibly go to prison, would you take the blame?"

Silence filled the line. "Jaysus, Biddy. Killed the fella, did ya?"

"No! How could you be thinking such a thing? It was merely a hypothetical question."

"Knowing you, I doubt it."

I piped up. "I guarantee you, if she was needing to bury a body, I'd tell you."

Collin heaved a relieved sigh. "Okay, I'd probably help you bury a body. Is that what you wanna hear?"

"Don't be needing help burying a body. I have Mags for that."

She was probably right.

"If I help you bury a body, I'd be making myself an accessory, so we'd both be going to prison," he said.

"Gee, how romantic. Doing life in prison together. If you're going to prison anyway, why not take the fall for me?"

I snatched the phone from Biddy. "She'll call you back later when she's not such a head case about the murder. Which again, we had nothing to do with."

"Thanks, Mags. That'd be grand." He disconnected.

I tossed the phone onto Biddy's bed. "If you're looking for a reason to mess things up with Collin, I'd focus on the fact that he believed *me*, not *you*, that you hadn't killed someone."

Biddy sat there wearing a goofy grin. "A fella has never offered to help me bury a body."

Time for the happy couple to pick out Queen Victoria china patterns.

Fifteen

THE NEXT MORNING we decided to skip breakfast. My stomach was too queasy to eat. Biddy ate a buttery from my breakfast stash while we prepared our plan to prove Garrett Maxwell killed Malcolm.

"I'll pretend like I know what his and Malcolm's argument was about a few hours before the murder," I said, walking out our guest room door. "We need to somehow get Garrett to slip up and admit his guilt."

"That isn't going to be easy when Ian has confessed."

"If that fails, then we have to get in to see Charlotte at the clinic. She wouldn't have run off if she didn't have something to hide. No way she admitted herself because she was traumatized finding a dead body, when she wanted to pull an arrow from it."

Arguing echoed up the open staircase. Was one peaceful morning too much to ask? It sounded like our delivery friend Alec. Biddy and I flew down the stairs. We arrived at Izzy's room as she slammed the door shut in Alec's face.

Alec snatched a ring off the red carpet. "She didn't return

this the other day with the rest of her purchases. The shop's manager offered me fifty quid to get it back." He wore a triumphant grin, holding up the emerald and diamond ring sparkling in the light.

"Isn't that her engagement ring?" I said.

Biddy nodded. "It certainly is."

"Nay," Alec said. "I brought it with my first deliveries the morning after the bloke died."

"Are you sure about that?" I said.

He nodded. "Best get it back to the shop."

"Just a sec." I snapped a pic of the ring in case I needed evidence. Ava and Rhona had also witnessed the supposed engagement ring on Izzy's finger.

Alec trotted down the stairs. We trailed behind until the second floor, where we slipped into the unoccupied library lounge.

"Izzy lied about the engagement?" Biddy said. "No way did a ring from Chloe's cost seven thousand pounds. Not to mention, Malcolm couldn't have slipped the ring on her finger, because he was already dead by the time she received it."

"Being engaged made her look innocent. She had no reason to murder her fiancé, unless he wasn't her fiancé. And never would be. Maybe Izzy gave Malcolm an ultimatum that he had to leave his wife and marry her. And he said *sorry— this was fun while it lasted, but I have no plans to marry some hussy.*"

"Or she found out he was broke, and there went her sugar daddy. She wigged out and shot him with an arrow."

"That would mean she knew about the arrow." I tapped a finger against my lips. "If Lily is right and Malcolm stole it, maybe he'd hidden it in Izzy's suite. If she does indeed know where Malcolm stashed money away, that's one more motive."

"Yet if Malcolm told Izzy he wasn't marrying her, wouldn't she have threatened to tell the police he'd stolen the arrow?"

"It was her word against his. Maybe he threatened to expose her as the thief. Even broke, he could have hired a better lawyer than Izzy could have. We need to prove the entire engagement was staged, including the champagne."

"Can't believe we bought that bloody story about a romantic wedding in Tuscany and Malcolm buying her a villa for a wedding present. She must have spent all night making that up. I can't remember the name of the villa, but I'll certainly know it when I see it." Biddy searched the web for Tuscany wedding venues until Izzy's popped up. "Bingo." She called the event planner listed on the website. In her voice mail message, Biddy pretended to be Izzy wanting to schedule an appointment to tour the venue for her spring wedding.

We raced down the stairs to the registration desk. Lily verified that Izzy had ordered the champagne from room service the morning after Malcolm's death. Might have seemed too obvious to have ordered it the evening he died. She hadn't thought that anyone would check to see when she'd placed it.

"It's all my fault that innocent man is in jail," Lily said. "When it should be Garrett Maxwell going to prison."

"Shhh." I placed my finger to my lips. I glanced around, making sure Garrett wasn't lurking in the shadows, then leaned in toward Lily and lowered my voice. "You haven't told anyone our theory that Garrett might be guilty, have you?"

Lily glanced down at her desk, nibbling on her lip. "Nay."

"Who'd you tell?" Biddy demanded.

"Just my mum. I told her not to ring Auntie Julia, who can't keep a secret."

"Can your mum keep a secret?" Biddy asked.

Lily's vigorous nodding ended with a shrug.

"Ah, that's just grand." Biddy's gaze darted to me. "Now if he isn't guilty, he'll be suing us for defamation of character."

Lily's nose crinkled. "Not guilty? I thought he was?"

"Again, it's merely a theory," I said. "We need to keep an open mind right now. That's why we're looking into other suspects."

Lily's eyes widened. "You think Izzy was in on it with Garrett?"

"We can't give out any details at this point."

What details were left to share?

"She had me reserve a car to collect her at noon."

"Don't let her leave," Biddy said.

"Call the driver and push her pickup back an hour without telling her, or she'll get a taxi."

Lily nodded, snatching up the phone.

We asked her to also call us a taxi. We headed out the front entrance to wait for our ride to the police station to fill Detective Henderson in on our suspicions. We sat on a wooden bench.

"This isn't a lot of evidence, but perhaps the police can at least detain—"

"Me?" Garrett Maxwell said, appearing out of nowhere.

Biddy and I let out a squeal and snapped back against the bench.

"In case you didn't hear, Ian Murray confessed to the murder," he said.

I swallowed the lump of panic in my throat. "That's doesn't mean he did it."

A crazy look filled his brown eyes. "Aye, that's indeed what it means. You two lassies need to stop talking about things you know nothing about."

I squared my shoulders, heart thumping. "Like your argument with Malcolm in the garden?" I held the man's sinister gaze.

"I figured it was you who'd told the detective."

"I heard everything. I was holding back telling the police all of it until the time was right."

"Go ahead. Knowing Malcolm nicked the arrow doesn't make me a killer. I gave him an ultimatum. To return it or I was going to the police. That's what the argument was about." His devious grin challenged me to prove otherwise.

"Yeah, right," Biddy spat. "You wanted a cut of the sale, and Malcolm refused."

The man's eyes went from crazy to certifiable. He leaned in, mere inches from Biddy's face. "Prove it. It's my word against a dead man's."

A taxi pulled up the drive.

Biddy's bravado flew out the window, and she raced toward the arriving vehicle.

I surged to my feet, nearly crashing into Garrett's chest. Knees shaking, I stood my ground. "We don't have time for this. We're too busy proving who murdered Malcolm. And as much as I wish it were you, I don't think it is." He was now second on my list of suspects, right after Izzy.

Garrett looked skeptical.

I darted around him and hopped into the backseat next to Biddy. "I cannot believe you just left me there with that psycho. And here I'd been prepared to bury a body for you."

The taxi driver shot a worried look over his shoulder. Not a smart thing to say when a murder had occurred a few days earlier.

"That was just a figure of speech," I assured the man, then requested he take us straight to the police station.

Gravel flew under the car tires as he sped down the drive. He couldn't dump us off at the station fast enough.

Biddy lowered her voice. "Garrett wasn't going to do anything to you while I was safely sitting in a taxi."

I let out a whoosh of air and collapsed back against the seat, still trembling. "I bet that's why Charlotte checked herself into that facility. She knew what was going on with Malcolm and Garrett. She didn't want to tell the police the truth—that her husband had threatened Malcolm for a cut of the sale."

Biddy nodded. "I'm guessing Detective Henderson knows her whereabouts. Wonder if he's been allowed in to see her."

"Even if the detective can't prove Garrett's involvement with the theft, I want it to go on record. I'm sure this won't be the last time the man's involved with something sketchy."

I hoped it would finally be the last time *we* were.

☘ ☘

The Dalwade police station was located down a side street where shops and restaurants gave way to a residential area. A white police vehicle with neon-yellow-and-blue panels sat in front of a stone building once likely occupied by a large family rather than criminals. We entered the station to find the young officer who'd slapped the cuffs on Ian sitting at the desk. He informed us that Detective Henderson was out.

"Do you know when he'll be back?" I asked.

"Said by noon."

"That'll be too late."

I quickly brought the guy up to speed on Izzy having staged her engagement. The villa in Tuscany had returned Biddy's call on our way to the station. The event planner apologized that the venue wasn't being held under Malcolm's or Izzy's name. When she offered to draw up a contract, Biddy said she'd call her back.

The officer shrugged. "Ally Quinn once told everyone we were dating. She claimed I was taking her to a dance because she'd never been to one. She was nice enough, so I ended up going with her."

"Ah, fair play to ya," Biddy said.

He smiled proudly. "Point is, the woman might have lied so she could say she'd once been engaged."

"She was married until just a few months ago to Tavish, the dead man's brother," I said. "She doesn't need to worry about being a spinster. Besides, she surely lied about her engagement to Detective Henderson. Giving a false statement is enough of a reason for him to detain her for more questioning."

He nodded faintly, picking up the phone. "I'll ring him."

"We'll go back to the hotel and make sure she doesn't get

away," I told Biddy. "Search for more evidence. Like if Izzy can even shoot a bow and arrow, seeing as she didn't participate in the archery event."

"Let's ask Ian. Maybe he knows and can think of some more evidence against her. We should also fill him in on our theory."

I twisted my mouth in contemplation. "Why don't you talk to him."

"Suck it up for the sake of the truth." Biddy's tone was more compassionate than her words.

The officer brought us back to Ian's cell. Heart racing, I walked past two cells to the far end one. Ian sat on a thin mattress, staring down at his brown shoes, looking exhausted and defeated. His five o'clock shadow gave him a more rugged appearance, like Tavish.

I skipped the pleasantries and shared our theory about Izzy having killed Malcolm.

An intrigued look filled Ian's bloodshot eyes, but he remained silent.

"So, you're sticking to your confession?" I asked.

"Aye."

"You honestly think Rhona is capable of murder?"

"Nay. She didn't do it." He rubbed his forehead. "But anyone is capable of murder given the right circumstances."

That was what I always said.

"Just like anyone might falsely confess to a murder to protect a loved one," I said.

"What you're doing is utterly romantic," Biddy said. "But it's absolutely mad to go to prison for a murder neither of you committed."

Ian gazed down, stuffing his hands in his front pants pockets, his confidence wavering.

"Can Izzy shoot a bow and arrow?" Biddy asked.

"Aye, she can. Tavish has a collection of bows and a target course in his backyard. She'd sometimes practice with him. When she wasn't worried about ruining her bloody nails."

Inspiration seized Biddy, and she grasped my arm. "When she saw Tavish at breakfast and slapped him, she broke two nails. She flipped out because she'd just gotten a manicure. What if she hadn't been referring to her manicure the day before? What if she'd had to get another one the morning after Malcolm's murder?"

I nodded. "And why would she have needed another one when she'd just had one the day of the archery event? Not like she participated in it. She's super careful of her nails except when she isn't thinking rationally. Like when she slapped Tavish and when she nearly took your eye out. And when she killed Malcolm."

"Discovering she chose Malcolm over Tavish only to learn he was broke could certainly have sent her over the edge," Biddy said.

"I need to tell you something." Ian wore a hesitant look before continuing. "Rhona came to see me this morning. She was packing and realized that Malcolm's bow case was empty."

My eyes widened. "Malcolm's bow is missing?"

He nodded. "Aye, I found that a bit odd. And incriminating. Told Rhona not to be mentioning it to anyone."

"What if Malcolm went to Izzy's room after the archery competition and left his bow there?" I said. "Besides motive, we now have means."

"We need to find that bow." Biddy peered over at Ian. "Hang in there."

Ian nodded. "Thanks for what you lassies are doing."

"I'm merely doing what's right," I said. "My dad instilled a strong code of ethics in me."

Nothing like hitting the man when he was already down.

Yet I was down too, without having any choice in the matter!

Sixteen

UPON ARRIVING BACK at the hotel, we headed straight to the spa, located down a winding hall from the library. We entered the tranquil oasis, and the calming light-gray walls and lavender-citrus scent eased my tension. A young woman in an aqua-colored uniform, sitting behind a desk, greeted us with a smile.

The manicurist who'd done Izzy's nails the day after Malcolm's death had also done Biddy's. Between appointments, the middle-aged redhead was sitting in the back drinking cucumber water and watching the soap opera *Coronation Street*. We tactfully inquired about Izzy's nails, not wanting rumors of her suspected guilt getting back to the woman before we'd compiled all the evidence.

"I love her nail color," I told the woman. "Do you sell the polish here?"

She nodded. "Candy Apple. I can grab you a bottle."

"You did a fab job repairing all the broken nails she's had the past few days," Biddy said.

"The two the other morning took off a bit of skin on her fingers." The woman winced.

"Painful when she's right handed," I said.

The woman nodded.

The hand that would have pulled the string.

"Poor hen. She also had quite the bruise on her other forearm. I noticed it when I was massaging her hands and lower arms. She said it happened at an archery event."

A team-building event she hadn't participated in.

Biddy placed a hand to her bruised chest. "That's grand you were able to get her in last minute."

"Aye. It wasn't on the schedule when I left the day before. She must have made it with the hotel's registration desk."

"I was surprised she kept the appointment."

If the man you supposedly loved was found dead, would you keep a nail appointment for first thing the following morning when you'd been up crying all night?

The manicurist shrugged. "Looking lovely makes people feel better in a bad situation. During an economic depression, lipstick sales skyrocket." She shook her head. "She was a wreck having just lost her fiancé—to a murder, no less."

"Her ring was quite lovely, wasn't it?" Biddy asked.

"She wasn't wearing it. Said it was too difficult."

She'd been wearing it an hour later when we'd seen her. Had she just received it from Chloe's?

Biddy and I thanked the woman and headed toward the spa's lobby with a bottle of Candy Apple nail polish. I'd dropped twenty-five pounds on a polish I'd never use and lavender-citrus lip balm. Maybe the balm would work wonders, like lipstick, and make me at least look like I had it together when my world was falling apart.

"See, the place smells lovely compared to the stench of death in the graveyard, doesn't it now?"

I smeared on the lip balm as we headed down the stairs to the registration desk. Biddy snatched the tube from my hand. She swept the balm under her nose, inhaling a deep breath, then swiped it across her lips several dozen times.

"Stop. That was crazy expensive." I grabbed the lip moisturizer and slipped it into my back pocket. "I'm sure Izzy got a string-slap injury on her arm because she was rushed to shoot the arrow. I doubt she practices all that often."

We arrived at the registration desk and asked Lily about Izzy's manicure appointment.

"Aye, I scheduled it 'bout a half hour before Mr. Murray was found dead."

"Did she make it in person?"

Lily nodded. "She came from her room in yoga pants and a T-shirt. Said she'd been working out."

Working out shooting an arrow and covering her tracks.

"You didn't see her go up the stairs shortly before coming down to make the appointment?" Biddy asked.

Lily shook her head.

"She could have used the secret passageway," I said.

Biddy snapped her fingers. "Brilliant. That has to be it."

"How would she have accessed it?" I asked Lily.

"The hidden entrance in the corridor was left open the day after the theft so Detective Henderson could access it as needed. With all the chaos, maybe it wasn't locked."

I nodded. "The detective surely fingerprinted the passageway entrances and exits after the theft. Where's the entrance by the back?"

"In the men's loo."

Biddy rolled her eyes. "No wonder we couldn't find it."

"When you walk in, there's a door that says *Staff Only*, so most people figure it's a supply closet."

Biddy smiled. "Sneaky."

"Besides the fifth-floor exit next to the Queen Victoria Suite, where do the other passages come out at?" I asked.

"The only other one that isn't gated—to prevent people from getting lost—is the one that leads to the library. The lounge closed at eight that night, so nobody would have been in there."

I glanced at Biddy. "She must have then gone up to her room and quickly changed into her negligee."

Lily handed me the key to the passageway entrance and two flashlights.

I glanced at the clock on the desk. "Only an hour and a half until her car picks her up." I peered at Lily. "Will let you know if we need you to push her pick up back even more. She can't leave here until Detective Henderson shows up."

Lily nodded. "Aye."

"And don't mention a word of this to anyone," I told her.

"Absolutely not."

"She needs to be leaving here in a police car rather than a Mercedes sedan," I said as Biddy and I headed out to the garden. "We need to find those two nails."

We reenacted the crime scene in the garden and determined that the arrow had likely been shot from a corner area of the shrub fence. We crawled around on the dirt path, noses to the ground, like a pair of bloodhounds. We swept our hands across the dirt in case the nails had become buried and trampled on. When that turned up nothing, we dug through the landscaping wood chips. Still nothing.

Biddy peered around in frustration. "How can the nails not be here? If the forensics team found them and considered them evidence, the detective would have solved the case."

"The secret passageway. Maybe she disassembled the bow in the passageway, and that's where she broke the nails."

My phone rang. Detective Henderson. I answered, and he agreed our evidence warranted questioning Izzy. He confirmed no nails were found at the crime scene or the passageway. However, he hadn't been looking for tiny nails in the dark tunnel. The passageway doors were dusted for fingerprints after the theft, but there'd been too many to narrow down one suspect. Archie had given several tours to family members. The detective asked us to detain Izzy until he could make it back to town in an hour.

"Fingers and nails crossed the evidence is in the tunnel," I told Biddy, opening the massive door leading to the back corridor.

We walked down the hallway dimly lit by natural light coming through the tall windows and the chandeliers with several burned-out bulbs. We came to the men's bathroom, and I rapped on the door, calling out. Coast clear, we slipped inside to find the *Staff Only* sign on a white painted door. I unlocked the door and opened it. I directed the flashlight beam down the stone steps into the musty-smelling abyss.

"Are you sure you're up for this?" I asked Biddy. "I could meet you on the other end in the library."

"No way am I missing this." Biddy eased out a shaky breath behind me.

Great.

We climbed down the stairs holding on to a hand railing,

a modern addition. I shined the light on the uneven stone steps and cautiously navigated the stairway.

"Euphemia," Biddy called out. "It's just us. No worries." She grasped hold of the back of my shirt, pulling the bottom of it from my jeans, startling me.

"Don't yell out to a ghost, then grab me."

"Sorry."

Thankfully, the stairs opened up into a bit wider passageway. An iron gate closed off the tunnel to the left, so we headed right. I swept the flashlight beam from side to side, keeping an eye out for rodents, Euphemia's ghost, and red nail fragments.

Biddy sniffed the air. "Do you smell that?"

"What? It smells like the cemetery?"

"No, it smells like Izzy's perfume. It's faint, but it's there."

I sniffed the air, inhaling the lavender-citrus balm on my lips. "Would the smell linger that long, or has Izzy recently been back in the passageway to find her nails or get the bow?"

Biddy came to a halt, yanking me back by my shirt, the collar nearly strangling me. I slapped her hand away.

"What if she frantically whipped the bow through that locked gate back there and had to return to get it?" Biddy gasped. "What if she's down here right now?"

I directed the light on Biddy's panicked expression. "How would she have gotten in here without a key? Besides, she's packing to get out of the hotel. And we need to get out of *here* before she bolts. We can always fib. Tell Izzy we found a trace of skin and blood on the bow she used. She doesn't have a clue we suspect her. Taken off guard, she'll likely crumble and confess or slip up and ask where we found the bow."

I continued down the passageway, and Biddy once again grabbed ahold of the back of my shirt. We hesitantly approached another gate, as if Izzy was going to jump out from behind it and yell boo! I shined the flashlight into the dark tunnel, and the beam landed on the face of a terrifying man. Biddy and I snapped back from the gate. Turned out it was merely one of several paintings. Wooden chairs, framed artwork, and other discarded items filled the tunnel.

"It's a dumping ground for old furnishings," I said. "If Malcolm's bow was disassembled, the fancy maple riser could have blended right in. The detective couldn't have searched back there because there's no key. The slip lock needs to be torched off."

"How would she have gotten the bow out?"

"Maybe she didn't." We stared in at the items, searching for anything that looked like the bow's handcrafted riser. Nothing. "She'd have needed something long to fish it out. Like...a rake or extendable tree pruner. That's why the shed was broken into."

"Yes! She'd needed a tool to snatch the bloody bow out from in there."

"I wonder if anything was missing from the shed. Doubt Izzy would have taken the chance of returning a tool, even if she'd done all this during the night. She might have broken her nails when breaking into the shed."

A short distance later we encountered a staircase. We climbed up the steps. I opened the door at the top and faced a wooden wall.

Biddy let out a distressed squeak. "How are we supposed to get out of here?"

I spied a door handle and reached for it as Biddy threw her shoulder into the wall. The door opened, and she went flying into the library lounge. It turned out the passageway door was hidden behind a bookcase panel. The bartender, taking a liquor inventory, gave us a curious look hello. We slipped the flashlights into our back pockets and brushed the cobwebs from each other's hair. We raced down the stairs and headed out toward the shed.

Seventeen

❧

WE SEARCHED the grass below the shed's broken window. No nails. The door was locked, so we pushed up the window. I laced my fingers together, and Biddy placed a foot in my hands. I hoisted her up. She scuttled through the window. After searching for several minutes, no nails were found. I helped her out the window.

I dropped my head back in frustration. "I don't get it." Peering around searching for answers, my gaze landed on the tree under which Izzy had been doing yoga. Not only was it near the shed but also a low-lying section of the castle with a flat roof. "What if Izzy was so frazzled, she couldn't get the bow apart? She couldn't risk running inside with it, even just to the secret passageway. Instead, she decided to hide the bow out here and come back for it later once things had cooled down. Of course, the passageway would be one of the first places the detective looked. But I bet he never looked up there." I walked over to the low-lying roof. "It's only a story high. She could have easily thrown the bow up there. Maybe she later broke into the shed for a tool to help get it down. She'd have put the tool back."

Once again we dropped to the ground near the castle and searched through the grass until we found the two red nails. Biddy and I did a high five. I wrapped the nails in a tissue and slipped them into my back pocket.

"They either broke off when she was tossing the bow up there or when she was getting it down. She never dreamed someone would search the grass for her nails. She could have later disassembled the bow and hidden the three pieces nearby where she was doing her yoga. Then when the coast was clear, she rolled them up in the mat and waltzed inside and up to her room without anyone noticing."

"That means the pieces are still in her room or packed in her suitcase."

We raced out to the entrance, hoping Izzy hadn't managed to flee. We made it there in the nick of time.

A black Mercedes pulled in and parked. We ran over to the car and stood in front of the driver's door, preventing the man in the black chauffeur's cap and uniform from exiting the vehicle. He rolled down the window and confirmed he was there to pick up Izzy.

"Sorry. She's running a bit late," I said.

He nodded. "Aye, Lily rang. I was already on my way so thought I'd wait here."

"I'm her assistant," I said. "Do you have Diet Coke and ginger biscuits for the drive to the airport?"

His gaze narrowed. "Nay."

I shot a nervous glance over my shoulder toward the castle's entrance. "Oh boy. Well, it's a good thing you're early.

My boss will flip out if she doesn't have them. She's a nervous flyer, and ginger calms her stomach."

"She'll likely get carsick without them," Biddy added.

The man's panicked gaze darted around the car's pristine black leather interior. "Any particular brand?"

"Flanagan's."

"Never heard of 'em."

Me either. Precisely why he'd waste time searching the store shelves for them.

The Mercedes pulled out of the drive as Izzy strutted from the castle in a pink cashmere sweater, jeans, and heels. "Wait," she yelled at the car speeding down the road. Letting out an annoyed groan, she dropped her Louis Vuitton bag on the gravel drive.

"He was early so decided to run a quick errand," I said. "He'll be right back."

"I'd have been down sooner, but there's still no bloody bellman on staff."

Or because she'd spent too much time on her flawless makeup and hairdo for the first time since Malcolm's murder. Nothing like getting away with murder to pull yourself out of a funk.

"We'd be happy to grab your bags," I told her.

"That'd be lovely, thank you. They're in the hall outside my room."

Biddy and I headed inside and up the stairs.

"We're hauling her luggage down four flights of stairs so we can search it, right?" Biddy said. "Not to be nice."

I nodded. "If it's not locked. Most airlines ask that you don't lock it nowadays."

Four matching pieces of Louis Vuitton luggage sat in the hallway outside Izzy's suite.

Biddy eyed the luggage. "Seriously? Had she planned to move into the place?"

Each bag exceeded the airline's maximum weight allowance by at least twenty pounds. We dragged two bags across the carpet and down the stairs, the luggage hitting each step with a thud. At the next floor's landing, we caught our breath, then shlepped the luggage into a small boardroom. Two bags were locked and two weren't. When we turned up nothing but shoes and makeup in the unlocked bags, we attempted to wrench the tiny locks off the larger bags without success.

Biddy was still tugging on a lock. "What if the bow is in one of these bags?"

I set the heaviest bag against a wall. "Too bad one went missing."

Biddy and I shared devious grins before continuing down the stairs with the three bags. We joined Izzy, tapping a shoe impatiently against the gravel.

Izzy eyed the luggage. "There's a bag missing."

"These were the only ones outside your door."

"Someone stole a bag in the ten minutes I left them in the hall? The crime at this place is out of control."

Yeah, thanks to her!

The sedan driver returned. "Couldn't find Flanagan's ginger biscuits, so I bought one of every other brand. I hope that's good." He stared expectantly at Izzy.

She gave him a baffled look. "Whatever. I have one more bag I need to find. I won't be but a moment."

The driver was beginning to load her luggage into the

trunk when Detective Henderson's blue car turned into the drive.

"Oh, here you go," I said. "You can file a report with the detective."

Panicked, Izzy tossed her carry-on into the backseat and hopped in next to it. "It's no big deal. Have the hotel ship the bag to me when they locate it." She slammed the car door.

Ship it where? The woman was homeless at the end of the month.

As the driver slipped behind the wheel, Biddy and I raced to the front of the car. The man peered through the windshield at us like we were completely bonkers. Detective Henderson parked behind us, blocking the Mercedes's exit. Izzy gestured frantically for the driver to go around us or run us down—I wasn't certain. She whipped a handful of money into the front seat.

Detective Henderson rapped on Izzy's window, which she rolled down. "Please step from the car. I have a few questions for ye."

Izzy smiled innocently at him. "You'll have to give me a ring. I'm going to miss my flight."

"Aye, you're going to miss a lot of things," he said.

Her smile faded, and she stepped from the vehicle.

We handed the detective the tissue. He unwrapped it to find two red nails. Izzy eyed the nails.

"Do these look familiar?" he asked.

"Similar to the shade I sometimes wear."

The detective compared the broken nails to Izzy's. "Exactly the shade, wouldn't ye say?"

"It's a popular color. I have great taste."

"Because they're your nails," I said. "We found them in

the grass near the garden shed."

"So what?" She shrugged. "You found two nails in the grass near the shed."

"The shed you broke into so you could use a garden tool to get the bow off that lower roof of the castle."

Izzy let out a nervous laugh. "That's quite the story."

"Not as good as your engagement one," Biddy said. "That had us going for quite a while, until we figured out you'd staged the entire thing."

Izzy rolled her eyes. "Seriously. I have a flight to catch."

I glanced at the detective. "I bet nail fragments and her skin are found in the string of Malcolm's bow, which she used."

Izzy's entire body appeared to relax, like we'd just hosed her down with the spa's lavender-citrus spray. "What bow?" Rather than an innocent question, it was more of a challenge for us to produce the bow.

How could she be confident we wouldn't find the bow if we searched her suitcases? She had to have sneaked the three pieces into the hotel using the mat, then up to her room...her room that had been sweltering when we'd visited her yesterday after she'd come in from the downpour with her mat.

"You burned the wooden riser in the fireplace," I said.

Izzy's features froze.

"What about the metal limbs?" I asked.

"Will we find them melted in the fireplace, then?" the detective said. "Or elsewhere? Even if we don't, I bet ye didn't think to wear gloves or wipe your fingerprints from the garden tool ye used to get the bow down from the roof."

Tavish sauntered out the front door for a smoke.

"Tavish, luv, you're just in time." Izzy gave him a pouty look, her eyes watering. "These two are trying to frame me for Malcolm's murder."

His gaze narrowed on the detective. "What's going on?"

"Push up your left shirt sleeve," I told Izzy.

"Absolutely not."

"Push it up," the detective commanded.

"The *left* one," I said.

Izzy reluctantly pushed up the sleeve and revealed a nasty bruise that made Biddy and me cringe. Biddy's hand shot to her chest.

"I fell on the steps. Hotel is lucky I'm not suing."

"Funny that you told the manicurist you did it during the archery team-building event, which you didn't participate in. Why would you have lied to a stranger unless you had something to hide?"

"Izzy, pet," Tavish muttered. "What have you done?"

"Not a thing." She shook her head vigorously. "This is ridiculous."

The detective eyed Izzy. "When we dust the garden tools, we won't be finding your fingerprints?"

Izzy teared up. "Malcolm stole that bloody arrow. When I found it hidden in my suite, he confessed he planned to sell it. That he was broke. But then Garrett Maxwell suspected him of the theft and wanted a cut of the sale. I'd waited two years for him to divorce his wife only to discover he's broke?"

Tavish's gaze narrowed. "Jeez Izzy, *two* years?"

Izzy frowned. "I'm sorry. I hadn't planned to kill him. But what if he got caught selling the arrow and sent to prison? I wasn't about to be married to a felon."

"Being in prison yourself was a better option?" Biddy

said.

"I refuse to say another word until I have a solicitor." She placed a hand on Tavish's arm. "Can you get me one, luv?"

He nodded, appearing more distressed over Izzy confessing to the murder than he had about his brother's death.

She wiped a tear from her cheek. "I never stopped loving you."

"You just love money more," he said.

Unable to contradict him, Izzy slipped into the back seat of the officer's car, assisted by Detective Henderson. Tavish watched the detective drive away with Izzy, massaging a thumb over the indentation on his ring finger. The Mercedes's driver bolted from his car, removed the luggage from his trunk, and left it on the drive. He sped off, likely on his way to give the scoop to the local newspaper.

"I know. I'm off my trolley, but I still love her."

"Enough to have taken the fall for your brother's murder if you'd known she was guilty?" Biddy asked.

He massaged his stubbled chin for a moment, then shook his head.

"Don't worry." Biddy placed a comforting hand on his arm. "One day you'll find a woman you're willing to do time for."

He arched a brow. "How about I find a lassie who won't be doing time?"

Biddy nodded. "It's best to set the bar high when looking for love." Her goofy grin was back. She was obviously thinking about Collin's offer to help her bury a body.

Thankfully, Collin had her back. Two dead bodies in a matter of a few months was more than enough for me.

Eighteen

TAVISH STASHED Izzy's expensive designer luggage in his car. He planned to pack up her flat and put everything in storage. Even if he didn't love Izzy enough to go to prison for her, he still cared enough to look after her. Maybe, like Ava's guilt over having introduced her best friend to Malcolm, Tavish carried some weird sense of responsibility for introducing his slutty wife to his brother. I was relieved to not be in a relationship.

Biddy went up to pack while I popped by Dad's room and filled him in on what had happened.

He shook his head in disapproval. "Didn't I tell you to share your theory with Detective Henderson and allow him to handle the matter?"

I nodded.

His stern look softened. "I guess it's a good thing you don't always listen to your father." He gave me a big hug, then drew back, his eyes watering. "I'm so proud of you. You've become such a strong and independent woman. I knew you would. You were only five when you snuck out of your kindergarten class and walked home to check on me when I was sick. You didn't think I should be home alone when I wasn't feeling well. It was only three blocks away, but still."

That was my earliest childhood memory.

"Would you like to wait around and talk to Ian once he's released?"

"No. I'm still not sure what to say to him. I need time away from this castle and Scotland to clear my head. Besides, I'd like to get to the hotel in Edinburgh in time to go out for dinner."

"Would it have been better if your biological father had turned out to be some random man your mom spent one night with?"

"Maybe. That way it wouldn't ruin your relationship with Ian."

"Ian and I will work through this. It's you I'm worried about."

"I wanted to identify my biological father but wasn't sure if I'd ever even contact him. I assumed I'd have time to process the discovery and that meeting him would be on my terms."

"Unfortunately, life doesn't always happen on our terms. What if it had ended up being Malcolm?"

I cringed. "I get it. I could have done a lot worse, but that still doesn't make it easy."

"I know. None of this is easy." Dad kissed my forehead. "Our car is due in a half hour. You want me to push it back?"

"No. We can be packed and ready to go."

I flew up three flights of stairs to my room, where Biddy was nearly packed. I tossed clothes into my suitcase but took a bit more care with the items going into my carry-on bag. I placed my Queen Victoria teacup in its box and wrapped it in my flannel pajama bottoms. I rolled my Clan Murray Scotch bottle in my pink Dublin Mudslide T-shirt. I strategically placed the items in my bag.

A rap sounded at the door.

My heart raced. "What if it's Ian?" I whispered to Biddy, who was zipping up her packed suitcase.

"You've got this." She gave me a thumbs-up and dashed to the bed nook and out the open window.

So much for a supportive best friend.

Taking a deep breath, I opened the door to find Ava and Rhona. Relieved, I invited them in. Biddy's arm reached through the window and grabbed the throw blanket off the back of the chair.

The women gave me curious looks.

"You can come back in," I yelled toward the window. "It's Ava and Rhona saying goodbye."

The blanket came flying through the window, followed by a shivering Biddy. "It's bloody freezing out there." She glanced at the two women. "That's our veranda."

"Maybe we can add it to the room description when we have the website and brochures redone," Ava joked.

"Might want to add a few outdoor chairs," Biddy said. "And maybe a propane heater."

"How about starting with a door?" I said.

Biddy shrugged. "We did fine without one."

Rhona handed us each a small box containing a Queen Victoria teacup. "With everything going on yesterday, these were the last thing on your mind. I owe you an entire set of china for what you did to help Ian and me." Tears of joy filled her eyes.

"Ah, that's grand," Biddy said. "Thanks a mil."

My extra one would make a perfect gift for Rosie.

"I can't thank you two enough, either, for proving Ian innocent," Ava said. "I hope you can forgive me for claiming Malcolm was your father. I shouldn't have blurted it out the way I did without more proof. I wasn't thinking clearly, having forgotten Tavish and Ian were with him in Chicago. Honestly, I wouldn't have suspected either of them anyway."

"No worries. I'll be fine."

"I hope you'll still head up the cemetery restoration project," Rhona said. "Tavish was telling us about some of your brilliant ideas."

"You think we're going to miss out on the opportunity to stay in a castle for free?" Biddy said, lightening the mood. "As usual, I'll be assisting Mags. I'm not expecting a *totally* free ride."

"I hope to forward you my plans in the next few weeks."

First, I needed to compile at least a rough draft for the upcoming *Rags to Riches Roadshow* Halloween episode. Maybe Kiernan Moffat would clue me in on the filming location so I could tie it in to the show's content. A haunted castle or stately home was my guess.

An eerie feeling slithered up my back over thoughts of once again working with the dodgy appraiser more so than the scary setting.

"Since the reunion didn't go quite the way any of us had planned, hopefully we can have a proper Murray gathering when you return for the project," Ava said. "One without any drama."

"A family get-together without any drama?" Biddy said. "How mad would that be?"

I turned to Rhona. "I hope Sienna makes it back okay."

"I'm picking her up at the Glasgow airport in the morning."

"I know how hard it is to lose a parent. If she ever wants to talk, have her give me a call." Thankfully, Biddy had been there for me when Mom died. I'd needed to at least appear strong for Grandma's sake, having lost her only child.

Rhona teared up. "That'd be great. Thanks. For everything."

It was weird. Suddenly I had a first cousin almost the same age as me. Not to mention an aunt, uncle, and two dads. I guess it was time to tell my sisters about my DNA discovery. Upon hearing my news, many siblings would rush to take a DNA test, worried about their own legitimacy. Not my sisters. I guaranteed they would rather have me be the only skeleton in the closet. Honestly, I couldn't blame them. If I had it to do over, I wouldn't have taken the test.

Dad was likely waiting for us, so we said our goodbyes.

After having schlepped Izzy's overweight bags down four flights of stairs, hauling our suitcases down was a breeze. Dad and Tavish were in the lobby chatting. No Ian. Had he not been released from jail yet, or did he merely not want to see me?

"Tavish and I were just talking about the northern lights," Dad said. "Am thinking about coming over in winter to catch them. He said cell and internet service are hit or miss." He eyed me. "Just what I need."

I smiled. "Yes, it is."

"That'd be brill," Biddy said. "Not to be inviting myself..."

"Of course you bonnie lassies are welcome," Tavish said.

I gave him a faint nod. That was great if my dad decided to keep in touch with his cousin, but I wasn't sure how I felt about exchanging Christmas cards with my uncle. I needed some time to let things settle so I could think clearly.

"Maybe we could camp out on *our* land," Biddy said.

"It's ten square feet," I said.

"Twenty. Remember, we're neighbors. That's big enough to pitch a tent."

"Do you think that's legal?" I asked Tavish.

He shrugged. "It's your land."

I smiled proudly. I was nearly twenty-seven, and I owned land in Ireland and Scotland. Who'd have ever thought?

Archie walked through from the registration area and placed a hand on Tavish's shoulder. "Have you heard the news?" he said to us. "You're looking at the castle's new archer."

"Temporary archer," Tavish said. "I agreed to fill in until another instructor can be hired. Not leaving my home in the Highlands anytime soon."

"I paid Charlotte a visit," Archie said. "Agreed not to press charges if she told me the truth about Garrett and her involvement with the theft. She admitted her husband had demanded Malcolm cut him in on the arrow's sale, or he'd turn Malcolm in for the theft. I'm giving them two days to pack their belongings and leave." He turned to Tavish. "You may decide the cottage suits you and prefer to stay on."

"Nay, I don't think so. Yet as an investor I'll certainly do my part to ensure the hotel's success. As will all the Murrays." He gave me a wink.

I smiled, yet my chest tightened at the thought of working alongside Ian when I returned in the spring.

Who ever imagined I'd visit Scotland expecting to take home a souvenir bottle of Scotch and instead end up with a family who were part owners of a castle?

Nineteen

By the time we dropped off our luggage at the hotel in Edinburgh's Old Town, it was time for dinner. There were dozens of restaurants and pubs within a short walking distance, but Dad insisted we take an Uber to one of Edinburgh's oldest pubs. He had checked a half dozen local beers off his bucket list, whereas I'd only checked off one cemetery.

Herriot's pub was established in 1560 and located in a supposedly haunted building. The same family had run the business for five generations. Over the years family members had added discarded belongings to the pub's collection, rather than a garbage bin. Keys, clocks, books, family photos, and even kids' drawings—which had likely once hung on the kitchen fridge—now hung on the pub's walls. The place was a genealogist's dream come true. Too bad we didn't have any Herriots in our family tree. None that I knew of anyway.

The wooden bar ran the length of the pub in the entry area. Dad ordered an unfamiliar Scottish beer, while Biddy and I tried a local cider on ice. We chose a corner table, and I slid onto an old church pew with a red velvet seat cushion. Biddy sat next to me, and Dad across on a padded bench.

I collapsed back against the pew, mentally and physically drained. "Can't wait to hit the hay, as Grandpa Murray used to say."

"This will revitalize you." Biddy tossed a glossy tour brochure on the table. City of the Dead. "I booked three tickets for tonight's tour."

I groaned. "Sorry. Don't think I'm up to taking a tour."

"You won't want to miss this one. The City of the Dead includes the Covenanter's Prison and the Black Mausoleum where the world-famous Mackenzie Poltergeist hangs out. The Mackenzie Poltergeist is the best documented supernatural case of all time. Books, TV shows, and loads of articles have been written on the place."

I perked up. "Which cemetery does it visit?"

Biddy rolled her eyes. "I'm talking about meeting a world-famous poltergeist, and you want to know the cemetery?" She smiled wide. "Greyfriars Kirkyard, which I know is on your cemetery bucket list, which you need to make a serious dent in. The tour departs in two hours from the Tree of the Dead outside some cathedral. That'd be a brill name for your family tree."

I smiled, taking a drink of cider.

Dad picked at the label on his beer. "All these cemeteries and Malcolm's death certainly reminds you just how short life is and you never know what tomorrow brings."

"I know where you're going with this," I said.

Dad wore a sly smile. "I don't believe you do. It just so happens I have an announcement to make. This is a bit of a celebratory dinner. I've decided to retire part time."

"Seriously?" I lowered the glass of cider from my mouth. "What exactly does that mean?"

"I need to reduce my stress. Add a few years onto my life expectancy. I'll do a bit of contract work, allowing me to pick and choose projects. Take time to travel. Spend time with you in Ireland and here, helping restore the castle."

"Fair play to ya," Biddy said.

I smiled. "That's wonderful. Maybe it'll work out that you'll be there in the spring when I begin working on the cemetery project."

"I think I can manage that, seeing as I'll be my own boss." He gave me a wink.

We clinked our bottles and toasted to Dad's new chapter in life. I wasn't yet ready to toast mine.

"Would be a good idea for you to reduce your stress also," he said.

"I told her she should have spent time in the spa," Biddy said. "A massage would have done you good."

"Graveyards are my spa."

"I'm referring to letting go of things you can't change and learning to accept them," Dad said.

"I knew this was going to circle back around to me and Ian. I just need time to process it all."

"What if Ian had been the one shot with an arrow rather than his nasty brother?" Biddy said. "You'd never have had the chance to get to know him. And if he's shot with one tomorrow, you never will."

"Why do I feel like I'm being ganged up on?"

"Not ganged up on," Dad said. "More like...looked after by those who love you." He reached across the table and placed a hand gently on mine. "Ian lives just two blocks from here."

Heart racing, my gaze darted around the busy restaurant. "So that's why you insisted on this place. You didn't invite him here, did you?"

Dad shook his head. "Of course not. He doesn't even know we're here. I want it to be on *your* own terms."

I took a drink of cider, and my heart rate slowed. What would I have done if he had been here? Left or locked myself in the bathroom? Or asked him to join us for a drink?

"Just thought I'd provide the opportunity for you to see him, but it's your choice. Rhona's heading to Glasgow to meet Sienna's plane in the morning. Ian mentioned he was going home."

A young waitress dropped off menus.

We scanned the dinner options.

"Here's your chance to try traditional haggis with neeps and tatties," Dad said.

My top lip curled back. "No thanks."

Haggis was Scotland's national dish, made with sheep liver and other unappetizing organs. The US Department of Agriculture had banned authentic haggis back in the 1970s. Why? I didn't care to know.

"What are neeps?" Biddy asked.

"Turnips."

Her nose crinkled. "I think I'd fancy fish and chips."

In need of serious comfort food, I decided on the same. The waitress returned, and Dad opted for the Shetland salmon with crab and vegetable risotto. We ordered another round of drinks.

A man walked into the restaurant, and I did a double take. The same height and build as Ian, but it wasn't him. What if this was his favorite local pub and he popped in? He was certainly in need of a drink after what he'd gone through the past week, especially the past two days. To top it off, I hadn't even hung around at the hotel to say goodbye. Something I was regretting. I polished off my cider and slipped on my blue quilted jacket.

"You just ordered," Biddy said. "Where are you going?"

"For a walk."

Dad smiled, giving me a wink.

Biddy caught on and gave me a good-luck hug.

"I won't be long."

Dad gave me Ian's address. Even though it was a straight shot only two blocks away, I entered it in my phone's map app. Being nervous and not thinking clearly, I might wander aimlessly for hours before I realized I was no longer even in Edinburgh. I stepped out of the pub, buttoning up my jacket, a cool breeze whipping my hair against my face. I headed up the sidewalk, passing by lively restaurants and pubs. The closer I came to Ian's, the faster my heart raced. By the time I stood across the street from a Georgian-style building with side-by-side townhouses, I was on the verge of cardiac arrest. I stared at the yellow door on Ian's place. He was likely in bed, not having slept well after falsely confessing to murder and then sleeping on the thin mattress in his jail cell. I probably shouldn't—

"Mags?" Ian said behind me.

Startled, I turned to Ian standing there holding a grocery bag. "Oh, ah, hi. We're having dinner at a nearby pub, and my dad mentioned you lived in the area."

He nodded eagerly, closing the distance between us. "Aye. Just across the street if you'd like to come over."

I shook my head, and his hopeful look faded. "I have to get back for dinner and don't want to miss our ghost tour."

"The City of the Dead?"

I nodded.

He smiled. "Good choice."

I held his gaze, unsure how to fill the awkward silence.

"I want to thank you for everything you did," he said. "Not just for myself but for Rhona."

I shrugged. "It was the right thing to do."

Not because you're my biological father.

"I'm sure you think I'm off my trolley giving a false confession."

"No, actually I get it. You really love her."

He smiled, nodding. "I do." He shifted the bag in his arms. "Edinburgh has one of Europe's top Christmas markets. Will surely be a difficult holiday for you, being the first anniversary of your grandmother's death. Maybe you and Biddy might want a getaway."

"Yeah, ah, I probably need to stick around home for Christmas. Be there for Grandma's friend Edmond...and stuff."

He frowned and glanced down.

"I'll be back in the spring for the cemetery project."

"You're going to do a great job with that." He set down his bag of groceries and peered over at me. "When I visited and gave you the T-shirt shortly after your seventh birthday, I realized your exact age. I questioned your mum, who swore I wasn't your father. I believed her, or at least I wanted to. I didn't want to break up your family over the one time she and I were together. I'd just lost my wife…"

I glanced away, watching a woman walking a small brown dog, which was happily trotting along.

"I'm sorry if it's too soon to talk about. But I have to tell you she regretted it. She'd panicked over the possibility of losing your father and her family if he found out. She realized how much she loved him and had to lose."

"Am I supposed to be grateful that your affair with her saved our family?"

"Nay, of course not. I merely want you to know our frames of mind at the time, and it was a one-off occurrence. I don't expect you to forgive me, but I hope…" He cleared his throat. "I hope for any time you might want to give me."

My eyes glassed over. "Well, as Biddy would say, I must crack on. Dinner is waiting." I turned to head down the sidewalk, then glanced back at him. "I'll see you in the spring."

He smiled. "That sounds perfect."

I wandered back toward the pub, the cool wind drying the tears in my eyes. I took a calming breath, a sense of relief washing over me. When I got home, I could remove the yellow slip of paper from the fairy house in my backyard. My wish to find my biological father had been granted. Who knew what our future together held? Yet rather than making a wish and asking the fairies to work their magic, I'd let nature take its course.

I had the feeling Mom was watching over me.

She had this one covered, rather than the fairies.

A Mags and Biddy Genealogy Mystery
Book Five

Genealogy Tips & Quips
Learn About Ancestry Research

Genealogy Research Tips

The following two genealogy research articles are from my nonfiction book, *Genealogy Tips & Quips*: "Truth or Dare: Are You Prepared for Your DNA Test Results?" and "Family Reunions: More than Potluck and Playing Cards." I am also including an article from my December 2021 newsletter: "Researching Scottish Ancestors in Ireland and Irish Ancestors in Scotland."

In 2018 I began writing a genealogy column for my monthly author newsletter about my personal research experiences. I was writing articles faster than I was publishing newsletters, so I decided to compile them into a book. *Genealogy Tips & Quips* includes fifty articles and two extensive case studies—one about how a paternal DNA test revealed my family's royal lineage, and my quest to uncover family secrets. I hope you find these tips helpful. You can learn more about the book at www.elizawatson.com.

Truth or Dare

ARE YOU PREPARED FOR YOUR DNA RESULTS?

What if you take a DNA test and discover you and your brother have no matches in common? However, he has matches with all your known relations. Shocked, you come to the conclusion you were adopted. You confront your parents, who deny your adoption, showing you photos of your mother's pregnancy a month before you were born. Now you are all baffled. Upon a closer look at your DNA matches, you discover two biological siblings. You reach out to them and learn you were born the day after their sister, in the same hospital. It turns out their sister and you were switched at birth. Are you happy about learning the truth, or would you have preferred to remain clueless and go on with life as you knew it?

I know several people whose DNA test results revealed this exact scenario and also ones who discovered they were adopted or that a parent isn't their biological one. I had a positive experience connecting with a cousin who'd been given up for adoption many years ago. And my dad's paternal

Y-DNA test revealing he isn't biologically a Watson, but rather a Burke with royal lineage, has been one of my most interesting discoveries. But not all surprises might be good. Before you decide to take a test, be sure you are prepared to accept whatever you might learn.

My dad and his closest paternal Y-DNA match have a shared common ancestor about six or seven generations back. Since I have confirmed my dad's paternal line back five generations through DNA matches, I was excited to learn their connection. I contacted the man's daughter, who manages his account. After we exchanged a half dozen emails, she was still baffled and said, "Are you suggesting our last name isn't Crowley? My ancestors came over on the Mayflower, so any name or lineage change had to have occurred prior to 1620. I guarantee it didn't happen in the past five generations." Once you go back five generations, or to the Mayflower-era, autosomal DNA tests become a gray area. That's when Y-DNA tests are especially beneficial. Many male surname changes occurred due to infidelity, adoptions, and other family secrets. Sadly, I thought it best to stop communicating with her rather than assuring her that Y-DNA doesn't lie. I was surprised by her reaction, but it demonstrated that many people are not prepared for the outcome of DNA tests.

When I was perusing a jail register in a county courthouse in my ancestor's hometown, I came across his name. Expecting a drunk and disorderly or a petty charge, I was quite shocked to find a woman had charged my married ancestor with sexual solicitation. A few months later, she filed a paternity suit demanding child support. Good to know. I'm now prepared should a descendant of my ancestor's illegitimate child one day appear as a DNA match. Even if I'm not as well prepared for other DNA surprises, I will remain open minded and go where the DNA leads me.

Family Reunions

MORE THAN POTLUCK AND PLAYING CARDS

Holding a family reunion is not merely a great way to stay in touch with family members you rarely see—it's a chance to meet new relations. When I discovered that my Flannery ancestor emigrated from Ireland to Wisconsin with his parents and four brothers, I placed an ad in his hometown-area newspapers inviting his brothers' descendants to the reunion. Several unknown local relations, and even a couple from Maryland, attended. The ad provided my email address, so several people contacted me in advance. I asked each of the newfound relatives to complete an ancestry tree so we could learn how they fit into the family line. I also suggested that they bring copies of family photos or email them to me so I could display them on a picture board.

A gathering is the perfect opportunity to bring out family photos and try to determine unidentified relatives. I regret not having my older relatives record people's names, even if it was with an ink pen on the front of the photo, like many of our vintage ones. Yet even photos with nameless relations are a treasured part of our collection and can make great conversation. I shared copies of my favorites with guests. Also, what better time to pass along your photos of loved ones no longer with you to their immediate family members?

While I was talking with a great-uncle at the reunion, he offered to drive my mom and me around the area to view old family homes. He showed us the rural neighboring homes where my grandma Coffey and grandpa Flannery had lived and first met. He shared stories about why the family moved to various locations. He pointed out the spot where my grandma's young cousin and his dog were struck by lightning and killed while sitting under a tree. This explained my grandma's fear of thunderstorms. I remember her reciting the rosary and burning palm leaves during wicked storms. Before I heard this story, her fear had seemed a bit irrational.

In another tip, I recommended a list of questions to ask your older relatives. You could send the list to them in advance and ask them to complete it prior to the reunion. However, it might not be completed in its entirety or to your satisfaction. I would ask relatives to answer the questions before or following the gathering so you don't infringe on their visiting time with family members. Rather than writing down their answers, ask if you can record them. This will expedite the Q&A process and give you an oral account of stories prompted by the questions.

Have a family-history corner offering photocopies of ancestor biographies, family trees, and picture boards. We also put together photo albums noting relatives' names, which sparked people's memories of the persons or the occasions, even some family folklore.

Request donations so you are reimbursed for photocopied items, invite mailings, and other reunion supplies. I don't expect to ever recoup the amount I've spent on research, but funds for the event are appreciated.

Have a potluck asking people to bring a favorite dish or dessert that has been passed down in the family. Following the meal is an ideal time for family traditions, such as playing a game of Euchre—a popular card game in southwestern Wisconsin. Have people stand up and introduce themselves and explain their family relation. Maybe a few will volunteer to share a short family story.

Before people leave, plan the next reunion. Have newfound relations provide their addresses for future invites. Ask people to volunteer for roles, such as creating and mailing invitations, printing photos, and assisting with a bit of research to get them more involved. Urge people to commit while their interest is piqued. Encourage them to reach out to you with information prior to the next reunion. Keep the interest and momentum going down through the generations!

Researching Scottish Ancestors in Ireland and Irish Ancestors in Scotland

The shortest distance between Northern Ireland and Scotland is merely twelve miles from Torr Head, County Antrim, to Mull of Kintyre, Scotland. On a clear day, you can peer across the North Channel from one country to the other. This close proximity made for easy travel back and forth by mariners, tradesmen, seasonal laborers, and others. After the Irish Potato Famine in the 1840s, many Irish immigrated to Scotland.

If your Irish ancestors had Scottish connections, you're in luck. Scotland's census began in 1841 and government civil records in 1855—and I've had great success locating church records dating from the mid-1600s. Unfortunately, a large percentage of Ireland's historical records were destroyed in 1922 when a fire ravaged Dublin's Public Record Office during the Irish Civil War. Ireland's 1901 Census is the earliest surviving census. Their civil records began in 1864, and church records prior to 1800 are scarce. However, I have a 1792 marriage record from County Westmeath, whereas the records I need for Castlebar, County Mayo, date pre-

1838, when that parish's records began. Tombstone transcriptions have proven very helpful in my Irish research.

How do you know if your Irish ancestors might be found in Scotland or vice versa? Look for hidden clues.

For example, in 1835 my paternal ancestor Mary Ann *McCarthy* was married in Ontario, Canada. In 1866 when her daughter Eliza was married, Mary Ann's maiden name was documented as *McArthur*—a Scottish surname. Canada's 1871 Census noted Mary Ann's origin as Scottish, birthplace as Ireland, and religion as Presbyterian—Scotland's national religion. My dad has numerous DNA matches with McCarthy ancestors from County Cork, Ireland, historically the area with the heaviest concentration of McCarthys. Yet I've been unable to confirm Mary Ann's family. Cork's church records begin anywhere from 1791 to 1888, depending on the parish. A few Protestant records date earlier.

Based on Mary Ann McCarthy's information, it's likely that her family emigrated from Scotland to Northern Ireland. So I searched DNA matches with MacArthur ancestors and found several from Argyllshire, Scotland. MacArthur is a sept of Clan Arthur from the county of Argyllshire. FYI, Mac/Mc were used interchangeably in Scotland. Sometimes within the same document. I am about to embark on tracing the MacArthur DNA matches forward, hopefully from Argyllshire to Ireland. Wish me luck!

In researching my mom's McDonald line, I've sent dozens of letters to McDonald descendants and obtained loads of obituaries and death records for McDonalds who lived within a twenty-mile radius of mine. I connected with a few relations, none of which had done nearly the amount of research that I had. When my John McDonald emigrated from Ireland, the ship manifest noted that a traveling companion, likely an uncle, was from Scotland. Unfortunately, I've had no success tracing the line back prior to John's birth in 1831 in County Kilkenny, Ireland. My mom has over seventy DNA matches with McDonald ancestors, mostly from Scotland. I hope to also trace this line forward from Scotland to Kilkenny!

In Scotland's census records, I often come across a family with children born in both Ireland and Scotland as well as an Irish-born mother. The Scottish father was frequently a soldier in Her Majesty's Armed Forces and was married while stationed in Ireland. According to my James Watson's military papers, he was born in Pollokshaws, Scotland. I've never located his baptism record or his parents' marriage record in Scotland. However, a James Watson was born in 1811 to a John (a common nickname for James) and Barbara Watson in County Galway, Ireland. The same birth year and parents' names as my James's. The father was a soldier in the Letterkenny regiment. I located an 1808 military record for a James Watson from the Pollokshaws area, who was stationed near Galway. I plan to review the regiment list when I visit the archives at the National Library of Ireland in Dublin.

Sadly, that James's baptismal record didn't include the mother's maiden name. James's mother's last name was Neil, and she was supposedly born in Scotland. Neil was an uncommon Scottish surname, whereas it was one of the ten most common in County Londonderry, Northern Ireland, where the Letterkenny regiment was located. From 1830 to 1850, 818 Neil baptisms took place in Scotland, whereas 16,555 were documented in Ireland. Since many Irish parish records weren't recorded at that time or haven't survived, the actual number would have been much higher. Same as Mary Ann McCarthy, James's mother, might have been born in Ireland to a family of Scottish descent.

Here's an interesting fact to keep in mind. Scotch-Irish is a term used mainly in the US and Canada to refer to descendants of Ulster Scots. In the early 1600s, during the reign of England's King James 1, Ireland's Ulster province (comprised of nine northern counties) was predominantly Catholic and the country's least Anglicized area. To tighten his hold on the Catholics, the king settled the area with loyal Protestants from England and Scotland. When the Ulster Scots later immigrated to America and Canada, they were typically referred to as Irish, since their families had lived in Ireland for nearly a century. However, after the famine caused a surge in Irish immigration, the descendants of Ulster Scot emigrants began calling themselves Scotch-Irish, not wishing to be associated with the newer poor and predominantly Catholic emigrants.

Even if you don't find hidden clues, if you've hit a brick wall with your research, look for your Irish ancestors in Scotland or Scottish ancestors in Ireland. You may well find them in both countries!

(FYI, facts on Irish surnames and surviving church and civil records can be found on two of Ireland's best genealogy websites at www.johngrenham.com and www.rootsireland.ie. Scotland's most comprehensive records site is www.scotlandspeople.gov.uk. An upcoming newsletter article will focus on genealogy research in Scotland.)

Author's Note

Thank you so much for reading *How to Spot a Murder Plot*. If you enjoyed Mags and Biddy's adventures, I would greatly appreciate your taking the time to leave a review. Reviews encourage potential readers to give my stories a try, and I would love to hear your thoughts. My monthly newsletter features genealogy research advice, my latest news, and frequent giveaways. You can subscribe to the newsletter at www.elizawatson.com.

Thanks a mil!

About Eliza Watson

When Eliza isn't traveling for her job as an event planner or tracing her ancestry roots through Ireland and Scotland, she is at home in Wisconsin working on her next novel. She enjoys bouncing ideas off her husband, Mark, and her cats, Frankie and Sammy.

Connect with Eliza Online

www.elizawatson.com
www.facebook.com/ElizaWatsonAuthor
www.instagram.com/elizawatsonauthor